A miniature su...
the Florida sk...

The accompanying explosion blistered the tops of the trees and reverberated like thunder in every direction.

A gust of hot wind hit the Executioner full in the face, and he turned his head aside to protect his eyes from the brilliant flash. The landscape was bathed in bright light that revealed every tree, every rock—and Bolan's position.

He darted behind the cypress again just a split second before a gunner opened up with an Uzi. Dirt spewed in his wake, and slugs thudded into the trunk. The instant the firing ceased, he galvanized into motion, continuing his dash to his car.

The warrior pressed his injured arm to his side to minimize the jarring. If his memory served, there was a narrow swampy area directly ahead. Once past it, he'd have a clear run across a flat field to the gravel road. He was almost home free.

At that moment a flashlight beam stabbed out of the darkness and caught the Executioner in its glare.

MACK BOLAN®
The Executioner

DON PENDLETON'S

THE EXECUTIONER®

FEATURING MACK BOLAN®

WHITE HEAT

A GOLD EAGLE BOOK FROM

WORLDWIDE.

TORONTO • NEW YORK • LONDON
AMSTERDAM • PARIS • SYDNEY • HAMBURG
STOCKHOLM • ATHENS • TOKYO • MILAN
MADRID • WARSAW • BUDAPEST • AUCKLAND

First edition January 1993

ISBN 0-373-61169-2

Special thanks and acknowledgment to
David Robbins for his contribution to this work.

WHITE HEAT

There is nothing incompatible between humanity
and a warrior's soul.

—Joseph Conrad,
The Warrior's Soul

An inhuman killing machine can never know the
meaning of those higher qualities that distinguish us
from Animal Man. A warrior's heart must never
grow hard. If it does, his days are numbered and his
soul is lost.

—Mack Bolan

THE
MACK BOLAN®
LEGEND

Nothing less than a war could have fashioned the destiny of the man called Mack Bolan. Bolan earned the Executioner title in the jungle hell of Vietnam.

But this soldier also wore another name—Sergeant Mercy. He was so tagged because of the compassion he showed to wounded comrades-in-arms and Vietnamese civilians.

Mack Bolan's second tour of duty ended prematurely when he was given emergency leave to return home and bury his family, victims of the Mob. Then he declared a one-man war against the Mafia.

He confronted the Families head-on from coast to coast, and soon a hope of victory began to appear. But Bolan had broken society's every rule. That same society started gunning for this elusive warrior—to no avail.

So Bolan was offered amnesty to work within the system against terrorism. This time, as an employee of Uncle Sam, Bolan became Colonel John Phoenix. With a command center at Stony Man Farm in Virginia, he and his new allies—Able Team and Phoenix Force—waged relentless war on a new adversary: the KGB.

But when his one true love, April Rose, died at the hands of the Soviet terror machine, Bolan severed all ties with Establishment authority.

Now, after a lengthy lone-wolf struggle and much soul-searching, the Executioner has agreed to enter an "arm's-length" alliance with his government once more, reserving the right to pursue personal missions in his Everlasting War.

PROLOGUE

Drug Enforcement Administration Agent Tom Carter glanced over his right shoulder at his pursuers a hundred yards behind him, who were no longer making any effort to conceal their presence, and increased his pace. Despite the reassuring feel of his service revolver in its shoulder rig, and although he only had two blocks to go until he reached his hotel, his apprehension mounted. He wondered why they were being so open about it. What did they know that he didn't?

Thunder rumbled in the distance, signifying the arrival of an evening thunderstorm in the greater Miami area.

Carter hugged the edge of the sidewalk nearest the street, where he could keep a trained eye on the traffic and scan the buildings to his left. He glimpsed his own husky form, his blue suit and blond hair, reflected in a store window.

Was the trio planning to take him out? If not, why else had they trailed him from Bayfront Park?

Carter derived some comfort from the fact that he was surrounded by pedestrians. He doubted the trio, or any accomplices, would be foolish enough to try to take him out in the open, but he knew enough from his eight years with the DEA not to apply any logical rationale to the modus operandi of professional killers. The better they were, the less likely they would adhere to a set pattern. Habits were luxuries only typical law-abiding citizens could afford.

A taxi horn blared abruptly.

Startled, Carter stiffened and almost reached for his revolver. He berated himself for being so jumpy. He paused for yet another look back and felt an involuntary tingle ripple along his spine.

They were gone.

Surprised, Carter turned and surveyed the street, checking every person in sight, every doorway and shadowed window. The twilight, combined with the darkening cloud cover brought on by the approaching storm, cast the grimy urban landscape in a somber grayish tinge.

The trio had definitely disappeared.

Carter debated his options. The wise move would be to forget about trying to reach the hotel. He should simply find the nearest phone booth and call in the information. The intel was too valuable to risk the delay. Better that the director learn the details immediately, and then he could worry about the lethal threesome.

A few large raindrops spattered onto the sidewalk.

His mind made up, Carter pivoted. His peripheral vision detected the slim figure standing behind him, and reflex brought his right hand sweeping up and under his jacket. As fast as he was, he couldn't beat his assailant's time. He saw the man's arm move and grunted when something sharp knifed into his abdomen and slanted upward.

"¡Bastardo!" the slim figure hissed.

Carter barely heard the remark. Shock threatened to engulf his senses. He struggled to maintain his self-control, but weakness already pervaded his limbs, and his knees began to buckle. He was appalled that he could fall to pieces so swiftly. An exquisite burning sensation flared in his abdomen and spread to his chest. He'd been cut before, but never like this.

The feral, malevolent face not six inches away suddenly moved off.

Carter felt the instrument of death sliding out of his body. He gasped and clutched at the rupture, his fingers slick with his own blood, and doubled over. The thought that he might die terrified him, and he offered a silent prayer that his life wouldn't end.

Grimacing, his consciousness spinning, Carter staggered against a wall and fell to his knees. He abruptly remembered seeing that malevolent face once before, in a certain file sent over from Justice. There could be no doubt about it. The Jaguar was in America, which meant the information the snitch passed on had to be true. Voices suddenly sounded all around him, and he became aware of pedestrians closing in.

Dimly he heard a feminine voice directing someone to call for an ambulance.

Soon help would arrive, but Carter knew it would be too late. An intense coldness radiated from the center of his being, numbing him. If he wanted to leave a message, if he wanted a small measure of revenge, he had to act now.

"Here, let me help you."

Hands gently gripped Carter's shoulders. He gritted his teeth and shrugged them off. Inhaling raggedly, he stared at the wall and raised his right hand.

"What's he doing?" someone asked.

With all of the strength he could muster, Carter used his right forefinger to write four words in bold red letters.

1

Someone else was on the prowl in the muggy Florida night.

A muffled cough from somewhere up ahead told Mack Bolan that he wasn't alone in the gloomy woods. He halted and crouched, listening intently. He estimated the sound had come from twenty feet ahead. As he was moving stealthily, he doubted the person had heard him. And dressed as he was in a formfitting blacksuit, with his face covered with combat cosmetics, he knew no one had spotted him.

A slight crackling sound indicated the person was on the move.

Bolan's keen eyes probed the darkness as he tried to detect a hint of motion against the backdrop of lush vegetation. The cough and the noise were the trademarks of an amateur, and he doubted that it was a guard from the estate.

The droning of the insects nearly drowned out another cough.

Now the big man had a fix on the other's position. He crept toward a towering cypress tree, focusing on the base of the broad trunk and the high weeds next to it. An inky form appeared, hunched to the right of the cypress, and he froze.

The figure unexpectedly shifted and straightened.

Bolan distinguished that the person had his back to him and seemed to be watching the estate. He glided warily nearer, a shadow among shadows. In his hands he held an M-16 to which an M-203 grenade launcher had been attached, the lethal over-under combo that had seen him through so many missions. In a shoulder holster under his left arm rode a 9 mm Beretta 93-R, a silencer threaded onto the business end of its barrel. Suspended on his right hip was a .44 Desert Eagle. Spare magazines and assorted deadly instruments of his trade hung from military webbing. Snug pockets in the skinsuit carried additional items.

The figure by the tree started forward.

Bolan closed, his right hand dropping to his combat fighting knife. He was eight feet from his quarry when amazement drew him up short. He'd detected the subtle swaying of long hair and registered the faint, unmistakable fragrance of tantalizing perfume. It was a woman.

She stepped hastily to the east, using every available cover.

Puzzled, the warrior crouched and watched. Her pale hands, clearly visible, were empty. From where he squatted he could see past her, see the gate situated at the southwest corner of the estate, and he realized she must be spying on Espinosa. He could only wonder what she was doing there, one hundred and fifty miles northwest of Miami in a secluded tract near the Everglades.

Moving rapidly, the mystery woman crept to within twenty yards of the high walls, to the very edge of the treeline, and halted.

A carpet of neatly trimmed grass and weeds extended from the woods to the walls, obviously maintained that way to afford the guards a clear field of fire. Spotlights illuminated every square inch of the buffer zone. There was no way she could cross it without being spotted.

The woman evidently believed she could, because the very next moment she darted from cover and raced through the southwest corner.

Bolan spotted a holster on her right hip. Whoever she was, she was asking for trouble if she intended to tangle with the sadistic owner of the estate.

Antonio Espinosa, according to the Feds, had left a string of bodies in his wake on his ruthless rise from the barrio to the top of his illegal profession. "Slick Tony," as one of his mentors had dubbed him years ago, delighted in disposing of his enemies personally. He'd developed a taste for torture and cruelty, and more than a dozen mutilated corpses found floating in the waterways of southern Florida were credited to his handiwork.

The Justice Department had been trying to nail Espinosa for years, but he hadn't been named Slick Tony for nothing. He used a complex web of fronts and covers that made tracking his activities next to impossible. On the few occasions when the Feds were close to scoring, their informants invariably vanished before providing the crucial information that would have slammed the legal lid down on Espinosa's drug empire.

Bolan had encountered many men like Espinosa in his war everlasting, amoral killers who snuffed out human lives in the same way they'd squash flies or mosquitoes. They were as cold as blocks of ice and deadlier than a nest of rattlesnakes, and destroyed the lives of countless others with drugs, guns or explosives, never caring who might be trampled under their bloody feet. And here was this mystery woman, attempting to penetrate the estate of just such a man.

The warrior straightened and made for the edge of the woods. He saw the woman reach the west wall and press her back to its surface. She drew a pistol and peered around the corner at the closed wrought-iron gate ten feet distant. He increased his speed and came to the spot where she'd halted at the treeline.

Holding her pistol in a two-handed grip, the woman inched toward the gate.

Bolan tensed. If she tried to go in by the front entrance, she wouldn't get two feet. His peripheral vision alerted him to movement above her, and he glanced up to discover a gunner perched on the wall directly above her head.

The smirking guard held an Uzi submachine gun, and he was in the act of aiming at the unsuspecting intruder below.

Knowing full well the consequences of his act, Bolan pressed the M-16 to his shoulder, took a moment to sight squarely on the target and sent three rounds into the man's chest.

The gunner danced backward, his arms flapping as if he were an ungainly bird trying to become airborne, and fell from view.

At the sound of the shots the woman whirled and crouched, scanning the woods uncertainly instead of hitting the dirt.

Definitely an amateur, Bolan thought, as he cupped his right hand to his mouth. "Run for it!" he bellowed. A glance along the top of the wall failed to disclose additional gunners, but more were bound to show up at any second. He looked at the mystery woman again and frowned when he saw that she hadn't budged.

Shouts sounded inside the estate.

At last the woman moved, sprinting for the trees just as the gate started to swing outward.

The warrior shifted to the right so he'd have an unobstructed view of the gateway, and it was well he did. A pair of hardmen emerged, each holding a revolver, and promptly spied the fleeing woman. They swung toward her and extended their handguns.

The raven-haired prowler looked over her left shoulder, saw the pair and tried to turn.

Bolan beat her to the punch. He drilled both of them, then stepped into the open and motioned with his right arm. "Move it!"

Predictably she hesitated, her apprehension transparent.

"They'll be after us in force any second," Bolan assured her. "If you want to stand there and be mowed down, that's your business." He backed into the shadows again.

The woman nervously bit her lower lip. Her features disclosed a Spanish lineage, and even when reflecting acute anxiety they were exceptionally lovely.

More loud voices rose beyond the walls.

Her mind finally made up, the woman dashed to the trees and slid behind a trunk. She stared at the big man without saying a word, then ran to the west.

So much for gratitude, Bolan reflected, and followed. He managed only a few strides when a commotion at the gate drew his attention to the six gunners who were exiting the compound. All of them carried Uzis, and half gripped leather leashes that were attached to the collars of snarling Doberman pinschers.

The big man took off. Dogs put the situation in a whole new perspective. He could elude guards easily enough, but trained attack dogs were another matter. In the dark, what with their black coats, heightened senses and superior speed, canines were formidable adversaries, ferocious and virtually tireless, able to rip flesh to shreds with their razor-sharp teeth.

"They went this way!" someone yelled.

Bolan raced to the west and swiftly overtook the woman. "They have dogs after us," he informed her while running alongside.

"I know, *señor*," she responded, breathing heavily.

"My car is a half mile from here. It's our best bet."

"Ours?"

"Unless you'd rather go your own way," Bolan amended, looking back. The Dobermans and the hardmen were nearly to the woods.

The woman skirted a bush before responding. "My van is almost a mile away. Will you take me to it if we reach your car?"

"Yes, but I'll need some answers first."

They fell silent, focusing their energy on maintaining the pace they had set, and covered over fifty yards.

Bolan's mind raced faster than his feet. The job had been blown all to hell, and Hal Brognola would be ticked off, but he didn't see where he had any choice. He couldn't just let that gunner blow the woman away, and now that he'd saved her hide from Espinosa's men, he was committed to getting her out of there in one piece. Slick Tony would get his soon enough.

A low knoll materialized ahead.

He started to go around it, but the woman went straight and he was forced to adjust his course so he could stick with her. A glance toward the estate revealed the gunners and the dogs had given chase.

The woman reached the crest and halted. She took great, deep breaths and doubled over, her hands on her thighs.

Bolan stopped, too. He realized she wasn't in any condition to run a marathon, and he opted to delay their pursuers, to buy precious time. "Keep going," he directed.

"What about you?"

"I'll catch up in a bit. Go about fifty feet and wait for me."

She straightened and nodded. "As you wish. But I must thank you for saving my life."

"Just get going," he reiterated gruffly. He watched her disappear in the trees, then crouched.

The hardmen closed rapidly.

Bolan knew they had fanned out, knew he couldn't possibly down all of them. He hoped to delay them long enough to make good his escape. The M-16's stock molded to his shoulder as he aimed the M-203 grenade launcher, approximating the impact point as best he could. Ten seconds later, when the pursuit drew within range, he fired.

The blast rocked the woods and was punctuated by shrill screams.

Pivoting, the Executioner went fifty feet and slowed, scanning the undergrowth, anger flaring when he discovered the woman was nowhere in sight. She'd skipped without providing a clue to her identity or her motives. Trying to catch her would be futile. Her van was supposed to be within a mile of Espinosa's compound, but in which direction? To the west lay the gravel road where Bolan had parked his vehicle. To the south was a highway, and she could have parked there and circled around.

He listened to a string of curses uttered in Spanish from beyond the knoll, then headed for his car. The fact that he hadn't terminated Espinosa, that he had zilch to show for all of his effort, for the two days he'd spent with Brognola going over the kingpin's jacket and plotting the strategy that would have put the psychopath out of operation for good, vexed him.

One thing was for sure. Hitting Espinosa the next time would be harder. The man was bound to increase security, probably even change his base of operations, which meant the Feds had their legwork cut out for them.

In another hundred yards the trees gave way to a wide field, and Bolan plunged into a sea of waist-high weeds on his way to the far side. What with his muffled footsteps and the swishing of the vegetation against his skinsuit, he didn't hear the new sounds until he paused to ascertain whether he was still being followed. His answer came in the form of savage snarls and growls.

The dogs were hard on his heels.

2

Hal Brognola rubbed his tired eyes, then stared intently at the telephone on his desk, as if he could make it ring through sheer willpower. He drummed his fingers for all of five seconds, then checked his watch. Again. Three a.m. Where the hell was Striker? Why didn't he phone?

A light knock sounded on the closed office door.

Startled, Brognola reached under his jacket. There was no reason for anyone else to be on this floor of the Justice building at such a late hour. "It's unlocked," he declared.

In walked a tall, lean man who carried a folder in his left hand. His angular features creased into a genuinely friendly smile as he laid eyes on the director of the Sensitive Operations Group for the United States Department of Justice. "Hello, Hal. Long time no see."

Brognola's jaw dropped in surprise. He relaxed, withdrew his hand from under his coat and stood. "Bill Keating! It's been two years, at least. How's the DEA been treating you?"

"I'm now in charge of the Resident Office for this part of the state."

"Then you're moving up in the world," Brognola said, extending his right hand. "Where are my manners?"

Keating stepped forward and shook, then took a seat. "I heard through the grapevine that you'd temporarily taken over Jerry Marcellus's office here in Miami, and I thought I'd pay you a little visit."

The big Fed's mouth curled into one of his patented scowls. "My being here is supposed to be hush-hush. How the hell did you hear about it?"

"I have my sources."

"That's not good enough."

Keating studied the Justice man. "You're making a mountain out of a molehill, aren't you?"

"No. I don't take security breaches lightly."

"It's not that sinister, I assure you."

"Then you shouldn't have any objections to filling me in," Brognola pointed out.

For a moment Keating hesitated. He looked at the file he held, then at his onetime friend. "All right. I don't want to start off on the wrong foot. But I won't reveal names."

Brognola waited expectantly.

"One of the Justice guys is dating a woman in my office. He happened to mention your visit to her, and she innocently related the news to me."

"Is that a fact?" Brognola responded skeptically. He knew Keating well enough to guess at the truth. Sure, the DEA staffer was probably sincere about her interest in her counterpart from the Justice Department, but he wouldn't put it past Keating to have tactfully persuaded the woman to reveal any interesting tidbits of information she learned from her boyfriend.

"I'm giving it to you straight," Keating assured him, wagging the file. "And if you don't mind, I'd like to get on to something else."

"I figured this wasn't a social visit," Brognola stated. "Not unless you've started pulling a night shift."

"I don't want anyone to know I came to see you."

"Do tell."

The DEA agent frowned. "You know how it is. There's been some bad blood between the DEA and Justice, and my superiors aren't too keen on their men requesting help from your department."

Brognola leaned back in his chair and cupped his hands behind his head. "What kind of help?"

"Did you happen to hear about Tom Carter?"

"Yeah," Brognola replied. "The story made all the papers. He was one of yours, I take it?"

Keating nodded. "A damn good man. Clean as they come." He paused, his features hardening. "Only half the story was printed for public consumption. The rest is the reason I'm here."

"I'm all ears."

"First I want you to be honest with me."

"With you?" Brognola almost laughed.

"Yeah." Keating leaned toward the desk. "Is our conversation being recorded?"

Brognola stiffened, feeling insulted by the implication. "You should know better. If you don't trust me after all we went through together, then you might as well walk out right now."

"I didn't mean to offend you, Hal," Keating stated, his tone conveying sincerity. "I just can't take any chances."

"Quit beating around the bush."

"Fair enough." Keating deposited the file on the desk. "Are you familiar with a scumbag by the name of Antonio Espinosa?"

BOLAN SPED WESTWARD, the tall grasses and weeds lashing his legs and threatening to trip him at any moment.

From the rear came a few short, sharp barks.

The Dobermans were gaining on him, and he knew he'd have to make a stand soon. He wanted to reach the next stretch of woods on the far side of the field, but it didn't look as if he'd be able to get there ahead of his canine pursuers. Killing dogs didn't appeal to him; they were, after all, simply doing as they'd been trained to do. But the warrior didn't relish the idea of bleeding to death in the middle of nowhere.

A throaty growl sounded close at hand.

Bolan whirled, drawing the Beretta. To his left the vegetation rattled and shook. An instant later a four-legged form charged into view and hurtled straight at him. The Executioner stroked the trigger twice and for a heart-stopping second thought he'd missed.

The canine killer kept coming, covering four more yards before it abruptly pitched forward and rolled to a lifeless heap at the big man's feet.

How many more had survived the grenade? Bolan wondered, resuming his race with death. At least one, he believed.

The sudden sound of padding paws confirmed his estimate.

Bolan tried to pivot to confront the Doberman, but he was already too late. A feral battering ram plowed into his legs below the knees and toppled him to the dank earth. Flat on his back, his arms above him, he saw the dog lunging at his throat and lowered his left arm defensively, trying to bat the beast aside with the M-16.

The Doberman bit down.

Acute pain lanced through Bolan's forearm, and he released the rifle as the dog shook its head furiously, its teeth sinking deeper. The warrior felt blood dampening his skin, *his* blood, and he pressed the Beretta against the beast's side and fired twice.

The Doberman let go, staggering backward. It uttered a final snarl of defiance and keeled over.

Bolan rose slowly, his left arm tucked against his abdomen. He replaced the Beretta in its holster and retrieved the M-16, grimacing at the throbbing agony that interfered with his concentration. Casting a cautious glance along his back trail, he headed for his car. Common sense told him to inspect the damage and apply a makeshift bandage, but he was disinclined to do so.

Time was critical. The dogs had delayed him long enough to enable any hardmen who remained in pursuit to close the gap. Wounded and weakened, he had to reach a safe haven quickly.

The warrior reached the trees and paused to get his bearings. A faint nose came to him on the breeze, a distinctive whooshing sound he was all too familiar with. The hardmen abruptly became the least of his problems. He had something worse to worry about.

A helicopter.

BROGNOLA HESITATED. Was it possible Keating knew about the game plan to eliminate Espinosa? Had he learned that the Executioner was also in Florida? He kept his features inscrutable and responded calmly. "I'd imagine that everyone involved in law enforcement in the Southeast has heard about Espinosa. When it comes to drug distribution, he's now numero uno."

"You've got that right. His network has attained frightening proportions. We've intercepted more than two dozen of his shipments and confiscated tons of dope, and we haven't put a dint in his operation."

"I know how you must feel," Brognola sympathized.

"Tom Carter was working on the Espinosa case when he was killed."

"Oh?"

"He'd managed to gain the confidence on an underling in Espinosa's organization, a man involved in Slick Tony's money laundering."

"Did Carter uncover anything valuable?"

"A few tidbits here and there. Then, a week or so ago, the snitch relayed information that Tom and I considered critical," Keating said.

"Don't keep me in suspense," Brognola prompted.

"Our informant claimed that Espinosa was getting set to expand in a big way. Tony told his people they would soon have to launder ten times as much as before."

Brognola was suddenly extremely interested. "Ten times?" he repeated skeptically.

Keating smiled. "I reacted the same way when I heard the news. Carter tended to believe his snitch because the man hadn't fed us any false information up to that point."

"Did this informant happen to say exactly how Espinosa intended to expand so drastically?"

"He didn't know, at first. Tom pumped him, persuaded him to do a little prying. We knew the risks involved, but we felt the intel was worth it." A haunted look came over Keating's face. "How was I to know?"

"So what happened?" Brognola probed, hoping to distract his friend from thinking about Carter.

"We hit the jackpot. We already knew that Slick Tony received most of his drugs from Ecuador and Venezuela. Now it appears that he's hooked up with someone who has direct ties to the cartel in Colombia, and you know what that means."

Brognola did, indeed. After Peru and Bolivia, Colombia produced more cocaine than any other country in the world. The Medellín cartel monopolized the production and wholesaling. Composed of the major Colombian traffickers, the organization had justly earned a reputation as the most vicious and feared criminal empire in existence. The cartel's members were always on the lookout for new inroads into the United States, always willing to take on new distributors. Espinosa, with his operation already in place and running smoothly, would be a prime candidate.

"As you already know, there are certain established transportation routes the cartel uses to smuggle their goods into the U.S.," Keating went on.

In his mind's eye Brognola envisioned the cartel as a gigantic evil octopus with its tentacles reaching out from Colombia into Central American countries and from there to the shores of America.

"If the informant was correct, Slick Tony is going into business with one of the major middlemen in Panama."

"Do you have a name?"

"Harmodio Remón."

Brognola whistled softly.

BOLAN IGNORED THE TORMENT in his arm and raced through the woods, skirting trees and bushes, listening to the chopper as it drew steadily nearer. If the gunners on board possessed night-vision equipment, they'd find him eventually.

He ducked behind the trunk of a towering cypress and expended precious seconds reloading the grenade launcher. In spite of his injury, Bolan succeeded in depressing the barrel release and inserting the new round. As he finished, the faint snap of a twig warned him that he wasn't alone.

Espinosa's hardmen were persistent.

The warrior crouched and scanned the vegetation to the east. The men on the ground had to have had radios, and once the chopper found him they would be guided from above. He had to hand it to Slick Tony. His security was tops.

A spectral form flitted between trees thirty feet away.

In the cool air above, its rotors whirring, the helicopter came closer and closer.

Bolan raised the M-16 and tracked the aircraft. Taking out the greatest threat first was an age-old military axiom. The trajectory would be tough to estimate in the dark, and there was always the chance of an intervening branch ruining the shot, but he had to go for the gusto and keep his fingers crossed.

Another figure materialized to the southeast and promptly faded into the undergrowth.

The Executioner breathed shallowly and kept his eye on the target. Even though the helicopter's running lights were out, its huge black silhouette was visible against the backdrop of stars. The blurred motion of its blades aided him in pinpointing the cockpit. He let the chopper fly uncomfortably near, then stepped out from under the spreading limbs and fired.

For a blazing interval a miniature sun illuminated the Florida sky. The accompanying explosion blistered the tops of the trees and reverberated like thunder in every direction.

A gust of hot wind hit the Executioner full in the face, and he turned his head aside to protect his eyes from the brilliant flash. The landscape was bathed in bright light that revealed every tree, every rock—and Bolan's position.

He darted behind the cypress again just a split second before one of the hardmen opened up with what sounded like an Uzi. Dirt spewed in his wake and rounds thudded into the trunk. The instant the firing ceased he galvanized into motion, continuing his dash to the car.

Bolan pressed his left arm to his side to minimize the jarring. If his memory served, there was a narrow swampy area directly ahead. Once past it, he'd have a clear run across a flat field to the gravel road. He was almost home free.

At that moment a flashlight beam stabbed out of the darkness and caught him in its glare.

3

The warrior threw himself to the right, out of the beam, barely evading the burst of gunfire that tracked him. He landed on his side and rolled, gritting his teeth against the pain lancing through his arm.

The flashlight went out.

Bolan distinguished a thicket ten feet away and crawled into it. To the south something moved briefly, then vanished.

The Executioner remained immobile, deciding to let them come to him. His plan was to let them pass by, then, once he was behind them, he could take them unawares.

Muffled footsteps gave away an approaching gunner.

Bolan knew that his pursuers had his approximate position pegged. All he could do was hope they didn't use the flashlight again. Without warning, a hardman appeared out of nowhere and halted fifteen feet away.

The man scanned the woods carefully, then shifted and motioned with his right arm.

A second gunner popped into view. They advanced together, each holding an Uzi.

The pair of killers came abreast of the thicket and paused, glancing about them, clearly confused. Finally they headed westward, proceeding with extreme caution.

The warrior watched them until they were out of sight. He had them where he wanted them. If only the third man would show himself... Inching along on his elbows, he turned and crawled into the open.

The woods were quiet and still.

Bolan placed his palms on the ground and began to push to his feet. He froze, suddenly aware of another presence. He didn't see the man or hear him. But he knew someone lurked in the surrounding forest.

In a fluid motion he surged erect and dashed in a zigzag pattern to a nearby tree. Once his back was flush with the smooth trunk, he peered at the vegetation, mystified. The hardman should have fired. Maybe there *wasn't* anyone there. Maybe he'd lost so much blood he was imagining things. He turned to go, and the movement saved his life.

The assailant stood ten feet away, his right arm arcing at the warrior's head, a metallic object glinting dully in the faint moonlight.

Bolan barely deflected the thrust with the M-16. He countered by swinging the stock, going for his adversary's face, but the man ducked under the blow and executed a flashing crescent kick that sent the rifle flying into the brush. Bolan went for his Desert Eagle and had almost drawn it when another kick slammed into his left leg above the knee. His leg buckled, throwing him off balance, and it was all he could do to snap off a shot as a third kick caught him in the left arm. Waves of pain washed over him, and for a moment the world spun. He extended the .44 in a reflex action. If his number had come up, he'd intended to take his killer with him.

But nothing happened.

The warrior's vision abruptly cleared, and he glimpsed his attacker as the man darted from view into a stand of saplings. Wondering what was going on, he turned and jogged southward, limping slightly. He couldn't understand why the killer hadn't finished him off. One thing, though, he was sure of—the rest of the hardmen would converge in the direction of his shot and be all over him if he didn't make tracks.

With the gunners to his west and the lone assailant to his east, he reasoned that his safest bet was to head for State Highway 82, then swing around to the gravel road and reclaim his car. Holstering the big .44, he gingerly probed his wound, feeling his fingertips grow sticky with blood. If he didn't stop the bleeding soon, the consequences could prove fatal. But he dared not take the time until he covered enough distance to provide a safety margin.

Bolan mentally reviewed the last attack. The man had been good, displaying exceptional skill. Only a fellow professional could have taken him by surprise, and only someone extremely adept at hand-to-hand would have taken him on armed with just a knife.

Or had it been something else?

Bolan shook his head, resisting a sensation of weariness that tugged at him. He had to be halfway to the highway by now. All he had to do was hang in there and keep his legs pumping.

The minutes dragged by.

Struggling to stay alert, the big man reflected on the fortunes of war. An hour ago he'd been on the verge of eliminating a devil in human guise, one of the countless amoral vermin who infected society with the twin plagues of drugs and rampant violence. He'd dedicated his life to removing such cancers from America's mainstream, to performing a sort of social surgery in order to safeguard the lives of those who couldn't fight for themselves and to prevent the disease from becoming worse than it already was.

Thanks to the mystery woman, Espinosa had earned a reprieve. A temporary reprieve, if Bolan had anything to do with it. As soon as his arm was well enough, he intended to finish the job he'd started. In that time, though, how many lives would be tainted by the poisons Espinosa dispensed?

The cost of chivalry had climbed since the Middle Ages.

Unexpectedly the vegetation ended and he burst out onto an asphalt surface. He halted, dazed from his loss of blood and strenuous exertions, and looked around as a metallic roar arose to the west. Headlights bore down on him, and he had the impression he was about to be rammed. Automatically he dived to the side of the highway and landed on his hands and knees. The exertion proved to be too much for his already-overtaxed system, and the swirling dizziness became a tornado that sucked his consciousness into a black void. Only vaguely did he feel his face strike the ground.

HAL BROGNOLA STARED at the telephone, then consulted his watch again.

"Is something wrong?" Keating inquired.

"No, why?"

"I get the impression that you haven't paid attention to a word I've said about Remón's activities in Panama."

The big Fed shrugged. "I'm just a little tired is all. My mind tends to wander." He paused and rested his elbows on the desk. "But I heard every word. You haven't told me anything I didn't already know. We have a file on Remón that's two inches thick, and we've wanted to put him out of operation for years. I'll bet you didn't know the CIA recruited a local triggerman in Panama City to pull the plug on him, did you?"

"No. When did this take place?"

"Shortly before the U.S. invasion. The Agency quietly eliminated a few prominent backers of the corrupt government, men who were dirty in their own right. But the *pistolero* they picked to take care of Remón botched the job. He was found floating in Gatun Lake with both his hands hacked off and his tongue cut out."

"Which emphasizes the point that Remón is every bit as ruthless as Espinosa. They'll make perfect bedfellows, so to speak."

"Let me ask you this. Are you one-hundred-percent certain that Remón and Espinosa have formed a partnership?"

"I'll be honest with you. Carter and I were skeptical at first. Remón has links to distributors in New York, New Orleans and Houston, but until now we had no evidence of his involvement in the supply lines into the Miami area," Keating replied, then frowned. "Thanks to Tom, I have the confirmation I needed."

"I don't follow you."

"Before Tom died, he managed to write four words in his own blood on a wall. Those words verified the intelligence."

Brognola leaned back. "The papers never mentioned that."

"We made damn sure the press didn't report it."

"What were the words?"

"Remón. Espinosa. Jaguar. Trinity."

"I can figure out the first two," Brognola said. "He was telling you that the two bastards have definitely linked up. But where does a jaguar and the Trinity fit into the scheme of things?"

A grin curled the DEA agent's mouth. "I thought you were familiar with Remón's file. You must have heard about his chief enforcer, the Jaguar."

"Who hasn't?" Brognola retorted, mentally chiding himself for forgetting. "What little there is to know."

The Jaguar was a legend in the circles in which he moved. No one knew his real name. None of the various law-enforcement agencies keenly interested in apprehending him had a reliable description they could use in tracking him down, and the only photograph believed to be of the elusive assassin had yet to be verified. The few concrete facts the authorities did have merely added to the man's mystique. A reputed loner, the Jaguar worked exclusively for Harmodio Remón. Whenever Remón had a problem with someone, the Jaguar took care of it.

"We think the Jaguar killed Carter," Keating revealed.

"Because of the name of the wall?"

"That, and the fact Tom was stabbed."

"Anyone can use a knife," Brognola pointed out.

"True, but the autopsy revealed the weapon wasn't an ordinary knife. It had to be double-edged and a foot long. Ripped the hell out of poor Carter. The internal bleeding was horrendous. There have been rumors that the Jaguar specializes in using just such a blade."

"What about the word Trinity?"

"We're still working on that one."

Brognola reached out and tapped the file Keating had placed on his desk. "What's this?"

"All the intel I've given you, and more."

"Why, Bill?"

Keating squirmed uncomfortably in his chair before replying. "What I'm about to say goes no further than this room?"

"Of course."

The lean man's face became a flinty mask. "I'll give it to you straight. I want revenge for Tom's death."

The revelation surprised Brognola, but he didn't let it show. "Oh?"

"Don't play games with me, Hal. I know you, remember? I know you have a wealth of contacts both in and out of government, more than I could ever hope to have. You're a man of influence. You get things done."

Brognola kept his voice steady. "And you want me to do the dirty work for you, is that it?"

"I don't care how it's done. I've gone behind my superior's back and handed over a copy of our file because I know you're the only man who can do something. The DEA has its hands tied, and if I took personal action, my career would be ruined."

"You know I can't give you an answer," Brognola said softly.

"I understand." Keating looked the other man in the eyes. "You're my only hope, old friend. I want Espinosa and Remón put out of business in the worst way." He paused, sorrow etching his features. "You, better than anyone else, can appreciate how I feel."

Brognola nodded.

"Good." Keating stood and offered his hand. "If I've overstepped the bounds of our friendship, I hope you'll forgive me."

"Don't worry on that score," Brognola said, as he shook his friend's hand.

Smiling in relief, Bill Keating turned and headed for the door, pausing on the threshold just long enough to check the corridor in both directions.

Brognola watched the office door close, then picked up the file. He thought of the torment reflected in the DEA agent's eyes and resolved to do everything he could to see that justice was done. Not the kind of justice involving courtrooms, lawyers, appeals, needless delays and eventual reduced sentences. None of that legal circus. The justice he had in mind was the kind that would put a permanent end to Espinosa and Remón's partnership, the kind of justice dispensed by the one man capable of making a real difference in the ongoing battle between good and evil.

The Executioner.

He frowned, glanced at the phone and addressed a question to the empty room. "Where the hell are you, Striker?"

4

A string of words echoed in Bolan's mind, rousing him from the land of the dead, and he listened to the conversation while struggling to control a feeling of light-headedness.

"—a lot of blood. Don't let him get out of that bed or you'll be rushing him to the emergency room at County General. I've done all I can do, Maria."

"And I'll never be able to thank you enough."

"Don't mention it. What are friends for?"

Bolan opened his eyes, feeling weaker than he could ever remember being, and discovered two women standing above him. The one on the right he remembered. She was the dark-haired beauty he'd seen at the estate. The other woman was older, a brunette wearing a white uniform.

"Remember, Nancy, not a word about this to anyone," the mystery woman said.

"Are you sure you know what you're doing? This man could be dangerous, Maria."

"I don't think so."

"You'd trust your life to a perfect stranger?"

"He *saved* my life. I think he's an enemy of Espinosa's."

Nancy's brows arched. "You still intend to go through with it?"

"Need you ask?"

"If I had any sense, I'd call the police."

Maria shook her head. "You won't turn me in."

"What makes you so sure?"

"Because you loved Carlos, too. You were like an aunt to him."

Nancy sadly bowed her head, her gaze straying to the warrior's face. "He's awake!"

Bolan tried to speak, but all he managed was a raspy croak. He licked his lips, determined to question them.

"You mustn't exert yourself, *señor*," Maria advised, leaning over and placing her right palm on his forehead.

"That's right, mister," Nancy added. "You need all the rest you can get."

"Who are you people?" Bolan asked. "Where am I?"

Maria knelt beside the bed. "All your questions will be answered in good time. For now I must insist you sleep. You have no idea how much blood you've lost."

"How long have I been out?"

The woman twisted and stared at a nearby wall. "Over eighteen hours," she said.

The news stunned Bolan. "I've got to make a phone call," he said, attempting to rise onto his elbows. The vertigo intensified and he sank down, feeling nauseous.

"Please listen to me," Maria pleaded. "I won't let anything happen to you. But you must stay in bed." She indicated the woman in white. "My friend works as a nurse. She knows what she's talking about when she says you might die if you don't lie still."

Bolan was in no condition to argue. He stared up into her green eyes and asked the question uppermost on his mind. "Why?"

"I'll explain later, after you've recovered."

There was no denying the concern she projected. He nodded, or believed he did, and suddenly sank back into sweet oblivion.

THE BLACK HELICOPTER swooped out of the east and angled toward the spacious backyard at the rear of the three-story house. Hal Brognola listened to the whirring of the rotor blades as he impatiently waited to land. He peered out the cockpit and noticed with satisfaction the federal agents swarming over the grounds. They would go over every square inch with the proverbial fine-tooth comb. If there were any clues to be found, the special team would find them.

A lone figure stood at the edge of the grass nearest the house, gazing expectantly at the aircraft.

Brognola surveyed Antonio Espinosa's isolated stronghold. Also enclosed within the four-acre area was a huge warehouse-type structure on the east side, and four smaller buildings to the north. Alongside the west wall was a long, narrow greenhouse. A paved circular drive connected the gate at the southwest corner to the front of the residence.

The pilot set the chopper down in the center of the yard and glanced at the big Fed. "Should I keep it running, sir?"

"No. I'll be here awhile."

"Yes, sir."

Brognola unfastened the safety harness, opened the door and stepped out onto the ground. He ducked his head as he moved from under the spinning blades, then straightened as the figure walked forward to meet him. "What have you got so far, Leo?" he inquired.

Leo Turrin's expression was grave. "You won't like what we've found, Hal."

"Let me guess," Brognola said, staring at the warehouse. "Slick Tony has flown the coop."

Turrin nodded. "The place has been cleaned out from top to bottom. Even the ashtrays were wiped clean."

"I expected as much after our bogus delivery-truck crew reported the place looked deserted when they drove by this morning."

"So did I. I sent people out an hour ago to scour the highway and the secondary roads, just in case."

"Good."

"Not so good."

"Why?"

"We found Striker's car."

"Are you positive it's the one he was using?" he asked, pondering the implications.

"It's the rental job he signed for using the code name you gave him."

"Damn."

"I've got teams out searching the woods between here and the spot where the car was found, but it'll be a miracle if they find anything in the dense growth."

"A needle in a haystack," Brognola remarked, and stared thoughtfully off at the far southern horizon. "We shouldn't count him out yet. There might be a logical explanation for his absence."

"Maybe."

"What's with you? Show a little faith."

The two agents from the greenhouse approached and halted.

"What's in there?" Turrin inquired.

"Nothing," replied the taller of the duo.

"From all the dust and cobwebs, it's a safe bet no one has used it since the previous owner, the one who was in the nursery supply business," added the other.

"All right," Turrin said. "Go lend a hand at the warehouse." He consulted his watch. "It's five p.m. now. Tell Phil we'll continue until dark and resume tomorrow if necessary."

"Yes, sir," the tall agent stated.

"I'm going to take a look in the house," Brognola said.

"Suit yourself, but there's nothing there to find."

"I've got to do something."

"Yeah," Turrin agreed, and sighed. "I know what you mean."

BOLAN AWOKE WITH A START, feeling disorientated. He sat up, trying to remember where he was. All he had on was his underwear. A lamp resting on a night table to his left illuminated a modestly furnished bedroom. To his right was a window; beyond, the tops of trees and stars. He stared at the foot of the bed and spied his savior curled up in a chair, asleep. Faint ticking drew his eyes to the wall clock, which indicated the time was one a.m. So he'd only been out for a few more hours.

Maria stirred, her eyes opening languidly, and the instant she realized he was awake she sat up and said, "Finally!"

The comment prompted Bolan to lean forward and ask, "How long have I been unconscious?"

"Since the last time we talked or all told?"

"Since the last time."

"About twenty-seven hours, more or less."

Bolan placed his palms on the bed, about to slide out from under the pink sheet, but a lancing pain in his left arm reminded him of his wound. He raised his forearm and discovered someone had bandaged it quite professionally. "Did you do this?"

"No, my friend Nancy did. Do you remember her?"

"The nurse."

"Yes. She cleaned and stitched the wicked gash you had. Then she came again this morning and replaced the original dressing."

"I'll have to thank her."

"There's no need. She didn't do it for you."

Bolan leaned his back against the headboard. "Oh?"

"No. She tried to convince me to take you out and dump you somewhere on the street. She believes you're trouble, that you might be no better than Espinosa, but she helped me because of Carlos."

"Who's he?"

"He was my son."

"Was?"

The woman averted her eyes. "He was my son, my only child, all that I had left to show for a bad marriage." She paused. "He died two months ago."

"I'm sorry to hear that," Bolan said sympathetically.

"Espinosa killed him," Maria said harshly.

"What?"

She turned toward him, the hatred in her eyes transparent. "That's right! Oh, he didn't walk up to my Carlos and shoot him, but he killed my son just the same with the poison he brings into this country. Do you know about the drugs Espinosa sells?"

"A little," Bolan conceded, touched by the depth of her feelings. "How did you find out about it?"

"I bought the information," Maria answered. "Used up nearly all of my savings, but it was worth every penny. I knew there had to be more to Carlos's death than the police claimed, so I decided to learn the truth for myself."

"How, exactly, did your son die?"

"The police say he overdosed on cocaine. They say he had to have used the drug regularly." She gripped the arms of the chair, her voice lowering. "But I know better. Carlos was a good boy. He didn't belong to a gang, and he never used drugs.''

"Then how did the coke get into his body?"

"I believe someone else put it there. Someone deliberately gave him the overdose."

Bolan pretended to be interested in his bandage, afraid his skepticism would show. Why was it, he wondered, that so many parents refused to admit their children might be on drugs? They would accept the fact that every other kid in the neighborhood was a junkie, but never their own. "Who would have had a motive?"

"The Diablos."

"Who are they?" Bolan asked, looking at her. By all rights he should reclaim his gear, phone Hal and get out of there. Instead he patiently waited for her to continue. There was a quality about her that appealed to him. Sure, he found her attractive, but it went deeper than that. Her sincerity impressed him. And there was something else he couldn't quite put his finger on.

"The Diablos are one of the biggest gangs in Miami, and they've been growing stronger every year. They started recruiting in our area six months ago. I found out that they tried to force several boys who live on this street to join, but they were turned down. My Carlos stood up to them and told them to go screw themselves."

"So you think the Diablos murdered Carlos in revenge?"

"Yes."

"Did you mention this to the police?"

Maria stood and walked to the window. "No."

"Why not?"

"What good would it have done? The police would say they needed proof, that without it they couldn't do a thing. Am I right?"

"Yes," Bolan had to admit.

"Besides, the way I see it, the Diablos aren't the ones to blame for my son's senseless death. The real culprit is the one who supplies the drugs to them and every other gang in Miami. It occurred to me that the gang problem in this city and elsewhere can be traced to a single root cause, namely drugs. Without crack, grass and the rest of it, the gangs wouldn't have the money they do to buy all those automatic weapons, fancy cars and whatever. They wouldn't be as powerful as they are."

Bolan thought her observation was a bit simplistic, but he didn't bother telling her. He noticed a closed door off to the left and slowly eased his feet to the carpeted floor.

"I decided I must do something about Carlos's death," Maria went on. "I couldn't let whoever was responsible get off scot-free." She glanced over her left shoulder, her eyes widening. "Hey, what are you doing, *señor?*"

"I want to stretch my legs."

She came around the bed in a rush. "You'll do no such thing. How many times must I tell you to stay still?" She placed her right hand on his shoulder. "Please don't get up."

Bolan felt the warmth of her skin on his own and tingled to her touch. He coughed lightly. "I want to stretch my legs."

"No. Not yet. You're still very weak."

"I can't stay here forever."

"But you haven't heard my proposition yet."

"What proposition?"

Maria locked her eyes on his. "I want you to help me kill Antonio Espinosa."

5

The helicopter flew low over the woods, almost skimming the treetops, and Brognola was tempted to instruct the pilot to take her higher. He changed his mind once he spied the wreckage.

"There it is," Leo Turrin said, pointing. "Exactly where the search team said it would be."

Brognola peered out the cockpit window at the charred debris scattered over hundreds of yards. He spotted the twisted rotor blades in a clearing and nearby a crushed section of the fuselage, both starkly revealed in the early-morning sunlight.

The pilot hovered to give them a better view.

"Striker's handiwork, maybe?" Turrin asked.

"Possibly." Brognola saw several federal agents moving about below, examining the crash site. He gazed westward and distinguished the edge of the Everglades approximately a mile away. To the north and south was more forest. To the east lay the estate. The nearest neighbors lived four miles to the southeast. Espinosa had wisely selected a remote site in the south-central part of the state for his base, and Brognola doubted there had been any witnesses to whatever transpired two nights earlier.

The trail was growing cold. The big Fed had to face the hard fact they were at the end of their rope. No clues to Bolan's whereabouts had surfaced, and unless they were exceptionally lucky soon, the warrior's fate might never be discovered.

The irony wasn't lost on Brognola. Mack Bolan had given his all for his country, yet no one would ever know about the man's sacrifice. Even the agents down below were completely unaware of the Executioner's involvement in the case. They believed it was a routine investigation, nothing more.

Brognola motioned for the pilot to continue and sat absorbed in thought. There was one man who possibly had the answers to Striker's disappearance, but Antonio Espinosa wasn't going to step forward and volunteer the information out of the goodness of his heart. For all Brognola knew, Slick Tony might have fled the country.

"Do we call off the search tomorrow?" Turrin inquired.

"If nothing turns up."

"Then what?

"I wish I knew."

"We could ask the Dade County Sheriff's Department and the Miami P.D. to be on the lookout for him," Turrin suggested.

"No, we can't. This is a sensitive operation, remember? We'll have to rely on our own resources."

"Which don't amount to squat at this stage of the game."

"There are a few things we can do. Have all the hospitals and morgues in southern Florida checked for a Joe Doe matching Striker's description. And while you're at it, have your team call around to all the warehouses in the metropolitan areas along the Atlantic and Gulf coasts. Concentrate at first on Miami, Saint Petersburg and Tampa, then work on the smaller cities and towns."

"That's a long shot."

"True, but Espinosa cleared out in a hurry. If that warehouse on his property contained a shipment, he'll need to store it somewhere temporarily until he establishes another base of operations. On such short notice, his best bet would be to rent a warehouse in a metro area."

"Unless, of course, he already has a backup base."

"There's always that possibility," Brognola admitted, "but we're at a dead end anyway, so what have we got to lose?"

"Not a thing," Turrin conceded.

The pilot suddenly cocked his head and touched a hand to his headset, listening. After a moment he turned to Brognola. "The search team has found something they think you should look at, sir."

"What?"

"Some landscape blown all to hell, and bits and pieces of a body."

Brognola's stomach churned. "Take us back to the estate."

ANTONIO ESPINOSA STORMED from the small office located at the rear of the warehouse in Miami's industrial district, his angular face a mask of fury, and headed toward a group of five subordinates who stood near a stack of wooden crates.

One of the quintet, a short stocky man, noticed the approach of their employer and whispered to his companions. All five stiffened and turned.

"Still no sign of those trucks?" Espinosa demanded, halting and glaring at the closed warehouse doors.

"Not yet, boss," answered the stocky hardman. "Anytime now."

"They should have been here already," Espinosa snapped, clenching his hands. "Eddy promised me by noon."

The stocky man smiled. "Relax, Tony. They'll be here."

"Relax?" Espinosa repeated angrily, and stepped up to his lieutenant. "Did I hear you correctly, Nick? You want me to *relax* after all that's gone down? Someone hits us in the middle of the night, gets right to the goddamn front gate, takes out five of my boys, kills my dogs, blows my helicopter all to hell, then escapes, and you want me to relax?"

Nick nervously licked his lips. "We got out okay, though."

Espinosa placed his right hand on the shorter man's shoulder. "You're missing the point, Nick. Someone was able to track me down. I don't know who, and I don't know why. All we do know is that a man and a 'woman were involved. Bruno saw them running through the woods.''

"Do you think they were sent to hit you?"

"Why else were they there?"

"At least we stopped them at the gate."

"It was still too close for comfort," Espinosa stated, and pivoted to thoughtfully regard the half ton of cocaine and other merchandise he'd been forced to load up and haul off at a moment's notice. He disliked being on the run, and despised not knowing the reason. The bimbo and the big guy, as Bruno had described them, could have been sent by any one of half a dozen aspiring rivals. He doubted the pair had been Feds or local cops; both would rely on SWAT teams to do their dirty work.

"Hey, boss," Nick said.

"What is it?" Espinosa responded absently.

"It's him."

"Who?"

"Him," Nick whispered.

Espinosa tensed. He kept his back to his men and listened for the sound of approaching footsteps, but heard nothing. No one could move that quietly, he told himself, and nearly jumped when the low, cold voice addressed him from behind.

"Mr. Espinosa?"

Fixing a grin on his face, the dealer turned and scrutinized the one man in all the world who made him feel inexplicably uneasy. He'd known his share of hard-boiled killers in his time, but never anyone who compared to the assassin who went by the unique name of the Jaguar. The name fit, though. There was a feline aspect to Remón's top man. In the way the Jaguar moved, in the soft manner he spoke, even in the steely glint of his green eyes and the contours of his features, the man resembled his namesake. He always wore a loose-fitting dark suit. Espinosa wished he would go back to Panama on the next flight out.

"Where have you been?"

"I phoned Mr. Remón."

"Why didn't you use the phone in the office here?"

"I wanted privacy."

Espinosa felt a flash of temper. "If I wasn't Remón's business partner, I'd take that as an insult."

"I don't care how you take it," the man in black said calmly. "And need I remind you that you aren't in partnership with Mr. Remón yet? The final decision won't be made until after I render my report."

"I just hope your report will be fair," Espinosa stated gruffly.

"Mr. Remón trusts me implicitly because I'm always completely honest with him. My report will be based on the facts."

"Facts don't always speak for themselves," Espinosa noted. "Take the incident at my estate, for example. If you're not careful, Remón might get the wrong impression."

"And what impression should he get?"

"That it was a fluke. Someone, somehow, got lucky and discovered where I was. I'll find out who ordered the hit, and the guilty party will be breathing water before you know it. It's obvious we're dealing with amateurs he—'' Espinosa stopped speaking abruptly when the man in black held up his hand.

"The man I fought wasn't an amateur. I could tell he was wounded, yet his reflexes, his speed, they were the equal of mine. He was most definitely a professional."

Espinosa suppressed an impulse to smirk. This Jaguar was the most egotistical son of a bitch he'd ever met. "And I suppose you told Remón all about the incident?"

"I filled him in briefly."

"Did you tell him you were shot?"

"No."

"Why not?" Espinosa baited him. "Afraid he won't think so highly of you if he learns you almost bought the farm?"

"My wound isn't serious."

"Oh, yeah? The doc said another two inches higher and you'd be worm food." Espinosa stared at the Jaguar's left side. "That must hurt like hell. How do you stand the pain?"

"I ignore it."

Espinosa marveled at the man's self-control. If *he'd* been shot just below the ribs at point-blank range, he'd take at least a week to recuperate in bed, even if the bullet didn't hit any vital organs or sever large blood vessels. Rather than praise the assassin's iron will, he decided to take advantage of the other's mistake. "I still can't believe you went over the wall without consulting me."

"There was no time. I wanted to observe the performance of your men, and I'd hoped to take a prisoner."

"You should have finished that bastard off when you had the chance."

The Jaguar sighed. "As I told you before, he used a .44. Although he only creased me, the impact knocked me backward, giving him a clear shot. The only option open to me was to take cover."

"But if this guy is as good as you claim he was, why didn't he kill you right then and there?"

"I don't know."

Espinosa smiled. "Sounds to me like you screwed up. Don't worry, though. I won't say anything to Remón."

"You're kindness is overwhelming," the Jaguar said flatly, and walked toward the office.

Filled with resentment, Espinosa stared at the man's back, wishing he could plunge a knife into it. He just knew the scumbag would give Remón a negative report, which would kill the most lucrative deal he'd ever tried to arrange. When he first sent out feelers to Remón, offering to become part of the Panamanian's network, he'd had no idea the heavyweight would send in someone else to inspect his organization. He'd expected Remón to come himself.

Of course, everything had gone smoothly at first. He'd put out the red carpet for the Jaguar, spared no expense in proving that his operation was a class act. He'd even let the bastard inspect his books. Success had been in the palm of his hand until the attack on his compound.

The thought caused his chronic temper to flare again. One of these days he'd find out who was to blame, and he'd personally carve the person into tiny pieces and feed the bits to a gator. He started to follow the Jaguar when loud pounding sounded on the corrugated metal doors.

"That must be Eddy," Nick declared.

Espinosa hoped so. He'd been forced to transport everything from the estate into Miami in a single truck. Now that he was about to move it all again, he wanted to divide the shipment among three trucks and send them on alternate routes to minimize the loss should the cops pull one over. He'd sent out his top driver more than three hours ago to find two more trucks, and the guy should have returned by now.

One of guards posted at the front admitted a pair of men.

"It's not Eddy," Nick said in surprise. "What are Felix and Hector doing here?"

Espinosa wondered the same thing himself. Felix Nunez was a middleman who distributed drugs to several of the gangs in Miami, and Hector Caro was one of the Diablos. He crossed his arms and regarded them critically as they came closer.

"Hola, Antonio," Nunez greeted him. *"¿Cómo está usted?"*

"Speak English," Espinosa ordered. Since half of his people were Anglos whose knowledge of Spanish was limited, he'd made it a standing policy to always converse in English in their presence. The practice fostered their trust, giving them the illusion he was always aboveboard and not hiding anything they felt they should know. Having them in his organization made good business sense. He knew from bitter experience that cops were less likely to be suspicious of Caucasians than Hispanics.

"Sorry," Nunez said.

"You'd better have an excellent reason for coming here," Espinosa stated. "When I called you to let you know that your next shipment would be delayed a few days and to tell you where I was, I didn't intend for you to pay a visit."

"I know," Nunez apologized. He was a tall man who had once been the leader of the Pagans, and he possessed a special knack for working with the gangs. "But I felt you should hear this in person."

"Hear what?"

"Well, you told me to keep my ear to the street and see if I could uncover anything about the man and woman who hit you, remember?"

"Yeah. So?" Espinosa said, lowering his arms.

Nunez indicated Hector Caro. "So here's the man who can give them to you."

6

Mack Bolan replaced the receiver and frowned. He'd hoped to contact Brognola, but his call to the Justice building had revealed the big Fed was out of the office and no one knew when to expect him back. So Bolan had left a message, using a code name and giving Maria's phone number.

"Would you like some more coffee?" Maria called from the kitchen down the hall.

"Sure," Bolan responded, adjusting the belt to the undersized red robe she'd lent him. He pondered the information he'd learned about her during their conversation the previous night as he walked away from the phone, debating what steps he should take.

Maria Salvato. Age, thirty-six. A divorcée who lived on Filisola Avenue in Miami, and who had devoted herself to the rearing of her only child until he was snuffed out at the tender age of sixteen by an overdose. She worked as a secretary at an accounting firm, and she was on a temporary leave of absence while she attended to her vendetta.

"The man I need to contact wasn't in," he commented from the kitchen doorway.

Maria glanced up and beamed. "Good. Then you'll stay awhile longer."

"I've already stayed too long as it is," Bolan said, walking over to a chair near the table and sitting down in relief. He still felt weak if he stayed on his feet more than five minutes at a stretch.

"Nonsense." She placed the coffee on the table. "You were in no condition to go anywhere, and you haven't recovered yet."

"I should have called him last night," Bolan stated, as he lifted the cup to his lips.

Maria shrugged and took a chair across from him. "You fell asleep again after eating the chicken soup, and I wasn't about to wake you up for any reason."

"Well, I'm not going to sleep again until after I contact my friend."

"Would you care for more bacon and eggs?"

The warrior gazed at the stack of dirty dishes next to the sink. "No, thanks. I'm full. The food is doing wonders."

"You feel stronger?"

"I'm not up to snuff yet, but I'm getting there. By this evening I should be as good as new."

"Don't push yourself."

"I know my limits."

Maria laughed lightly.

"You think that's funny?"

"I think *men* are funny. They're always trying to prove how macho they are."

Bolan grinned. "Is this the voice of experience speaking?"

"Yes. I've known my share, if that's what you mean. My husband, for instance, believed it was macho to pound me to a pulp once a week just for the general hell of it."

The warrior took another sip. "I've never equated wife beating with being masculine."

"Are you married?"

"No."

"Ever been?"

"Is this an interrogation?" Bolan rejoined, his mouth curled in a smile that didn't touch his eyes.

"No. Sorry. I didn't mean to pry," Maria stated, studying his face. She drummed her fingernails on the table, then cleared her throat. "Have you given any more thought to my request?"

"Yes."

"And?"

"No way."

"What have you got to lose?"

"It's what you have to lose that bothers me. You could be killed."

"I realize that."

"Do you want to die?"

"Of course not," Maria declared.

"Then give up the idea of getting revenge for Carlos's death. You're biting off more than you can chew."

Maria straightened. "I got as far as Espinosa's estate, didn't I?"

"And you were damned lucky I was there to bail you out." Bolan rested his elbows on the edge of the table and leaned toward her. "Listen, Maria. I'm in your debt for all you've done for me. If you hadn't found me and loaded me into your van, I'd probably be dead right now. I'd like to return the favor somehow, and the best way I know is to persuade you to forget all about Antonio Espinosa."

"And do I forget about Carlos, too?"

Bolan opened his mouth to reply, but changed his mind. Who was he to be lecturing her on the evils of seeking revenge? He'd launched a bitter war against the Mafia a few years ago for that very reason.

"You have no answer, I see," Maria said. "If you knew the pain I've experienced, you wouldn't try to stop me. To have the life of a loved one snuffed out by brutes who are no better than animals is a horror words cannot describe. I thought I'd had a rough life, thought I knew all about suffering and misery, until Carlos was killed and I discovered the true meaning of pain. Unless you've lost someone like I have, you can't possibly comprehend the truth."

Vivid memories flashed through Bolan's mind, memories of his father, mother and sister in happier times, before the tragedy that had altered the course of his entire life. He understood perfectly the motivation of this woman who had snatched him from the jaws of death, and he also recognized the quality of hers that so appealed to him. Their perceptions of life were the same. Both of them had forged an iron resolve to see justice done in the furnace of supreme adversity.

"Nothing you can say or do will stop me from going after Espinosa," she went on. "I know he's the main supplier of the poison that killed my Carlos, and I intend to make sure he's punished."

"And how will you find him again? He's undoubtedly cleared out of his place near the Everglades. In no time at all he'll be set up again somewhere else."

"I'll find him," Maria vowed. "If I have to sell my van and every other thing I own, I'll raise the money to buy the information, just like I did before."

"What's to prevent your source from selling you the wrong address?" Bolan asked, racking his brain for objections to her plan.

"He could, I suppose. But he told the truth the first time, so I feel justified in trusting him again."

"Who is this paragon of honesty?"

Maria swung toward him. "I see no reason not to tell you. My source is one of the Diablos."

"And you trust him?" Bolan responded in surprise.

"I'll admit I was skeptical when he came forward," Maria explained. "I'd been out on the streets for two weeks trying to learn all I could about Carlos's death, and one night I got a phone call from this Diablo who claimed he knew all about it and would tell me everything for the right price."

"He told you about Espinosa and where to find him?"

"Yes."

"It doesn't make sense."

"I paid him eight thousand dollars."

"Now it does." Money was the oil that lubricated the jaws of those who worshiped it. For a gang member, eight grand was the equivalent of winning the lottery.

"He also told me that Espinosa ordered Carlos to be murdered as an example to those who might think of opposing the Diablos. He said he wasn't personally involved in killing Carlos."

"Sure."

"I didn't believe him, either," Maria admitted. "But at the time, I was more interested in going after the big fish, not the minnows. To tell you the truth, I was astounded when his information panned out."

Bolan stared into his coffee, reflecting. The Diablo must have had an ulterior motive for giving her what she wanted. Perhaps the guy figured she'd be killed and no one would ever be the wiser. "Mind telling me the name of this guy?"

"Why do you want to know?"

"Curiosity."

"You're not thinking of looking him up and convincing him not to supply me with more information, are you?"

"How would I find him? I wouldn't know where to begin to look."

"True. And he's not very likely to risk talking to someone who looks like you, anyway."

"What's that supposed to mean?"

"You look dangerous. But don't get me wrong. I like the way you look."

Bolan simply smiled.

"As for his name, it's Hector. Hector Caro."

ESPINOSA SAT in the metal chair behind the small desk in the warehouse office and fixed his critical gaze on the Diablo who stood across from him. On the right side of the room were Nick, Felix Nunez and two other hardmen. On the left, as motionless as a statue yet the most commanding presence there, was the Jaguar. "So tell me, Hector. How is it you can give me the man and woman I'm after?"

Caro grinned nervously and glanced at the others. His eyes lingered on the sinister man in black, then focused on Espinosa. "Like I told Felix, I don't know nothin' about no man. But there was this broad awhile back who was stoppin' practically everybody on the street and askin' questions."

"What kind of questions?"

"She wanted to know who the big drug suppliers were."

Espinosa rested his arms on the desk and made a steeple out of his hands. "And why did she want such information?"

"I did some checkin' and found out she was the mother of a geek we offed for steppin' out of line."

"Elaborate."

The Diablo gestured and smirked. "Well, it was like this. Some of us were recruitin' in one of the neighborhoods and this punk stood up to us, bad-mouthed us in front of witnesses, told us to get out and never come back. So, naturally, we had to teach the dude a lesson. Some of us paid him a little visit."

"How, might I ask, did you snuff him?"

"We pumped him full of enough coke to make an elephant feel higher than a kite. Made it look like an overdose."

"How clever," Espinosa said dryly.

Caro laughed. "Yeah, wasn't it, though? And it was all my idea."

"I admire someone who has initiative."

"Hell, I'm full of initiative, Mr. Espinosa. One day I hope to move up and work directly under you."

"Do tell," Espinosa stated. "But back to your little story. Am I to understand the mother of the punk was trying to discover the source of the coke that killed her son?"

"Yep. That's what she was up to, exactly."

"And of course no one gave her this information?"

Caro laughed again. "Of course not. Who would be stupid enough to do something like that?"

"Someone did."

"It could have been anyone who knew about your place out there in the boondocks," Caro said. "I never could figure why you'd want to live out there with all those alligators, snakes and crap like that."

"Expediency."

"What's speed got to do with it?"

"Never mind," Espinosa said. "Did you happen to learn this woman's name?"

"Sure did," Caro replied. He wiped his palms on his jeans and fidgeted. "Not only her name, but her address, too."

"This must be my lucky day."

"I was sort of hopin' it would be my lucky day, also," Caro stated. "You see, Mr. Espinosa, when I got wind of the news about some bimbo and guy hittin' your place, I put two and two together and came to the conclusion the mother must be involved."

"How very perceptive."

"Yeah. Anyway, I figured you should be told. I was also hopin' you might see fit to, you know, give me some spendin' money for my time and effort."

Espinosa leaned back, his face inscrutable. "How much did you have in mind?"

"Hey, whatever you think is fair. You know how someone like me is always in need of bread." Caro tittered. "I like to party hearty as much as the next dude."

"I can well imagine," Espinosa said, rising. He walked slowly around the desk and halted next to the gang member. "And you have a deal. Give me the name and address of this woman, and I'll give you what I think is fair."

Visible relief washed over Caro's features. "Yes, sir. I knew I could count on you. Her name is Maria Salvato, and she lives at 2140 Filisola, a brownstone on the right side of the street. You can't miss it. There's a big potted plant on the stoop."

"You've certainly done your homework."

"I do my best," Caro said smugly.

"I'll send some men to bring the woman here. But first there's the matter of your payment."

"Yes, sir."

Espinosa was about to smash the Diablo in the mouth when a better idea occurred to him, a way of mending fences with Remón's enforcer. In a way, he was grateful that Caro had shown up. It gave him a chance to demonstrate his competence, to establish that no one pulled the wool over his eyes. It also explained the attack and conclusively proved his own organization hadn't been at fault. He turned and politely addressed the man in black. "Do you want to do the honors, or should I?"

The Jaguar's green eyes betrayed a flicker of surprise. "I would be happy to take care of it."

"Be my guest," Espinosa said, moving to the right. He was curious to see how the deed would be accomplished.

Caro glanced from one to the other. "What's going on here?" he asked anxiously.

"I am to handle your payment," the Jaguar stated, and stepped in front of Caro.

"How much will I get?"

"About twelve inches."

"Say what?"

Even though Espinosa knew what was coming and was waiting to catch the action, he almost missed it. The man in black moved so incredibly quickly that his motions were a blur. Espinosa saw the Jaguar's right arm sweep up and in, and at the very instant the right hand appeared to touch Caro's stomach the fingers curled inward and there was the faintest of clicks.

The Diablo reacted as if one hundred thousand volts of electricity abruptly coursed through his body. His arms were flung outward, his spine arched, and his chin snapped upward, his mouth falling open as he tried to suck in all the air in the office.

"This is your reward for your stupidity, *bastardo,*" the Jaguar said quietly.

Espinosa saw Caro start to convulse violently, and he clinically speculated on the type of weapon used. Whatever it was, it had to be wickedly lethal because already Caro's eyelids were fluttering, his body sagged, and he would have fallen if the Jaguar hadn't been holding him upright.

None of the others present uttered a sound.

Espinosa nodded toward the corpse. "This is what happens when you get too greedy. Remember it well."

"But why?" Nick blurted. "I mean, what did he do?"

"Haven't you figured it out yet? Who do you think told this Salvato woman how to find me?"

"The idea crossed my mind," Nick conceded. "But shouldn't we have proved it by beating the truth out of him?"

"Why waste our time?" Espinosa retorted. "There's no doubt in my mind." He glanced at the Jaguar. "Just drop the scum on the floor. My men will dispose of the body."

Slowly the man in black lowered Caro, who had gone limp, while drawing his right arm down and away from the body. A foot-long doubled-edged blade slid out, caked with blood and protruding from under the Jaguar's jacket sleeve. He began wiping the blade clean on his victim's pants.

"I've never seen a knife like that," Espinosa remarked.

"It isn't a knife." The Jaguar pulled back the sleeve, exposing a thin metal sheath extending from his wrist to his elbow. An inch above the wrist was a square spring-loaded mechanism that controlled the release action. "A renowned metalsmith in Brazil constructed this device according to my specifications. It has served me well for over ten years."

"I'll bet." Espinosa thought he detected a slight accent in the Jaguar's normally urbane voice, and he wondered for the umpteenth time about the man's nationality. No one seemed to know. His best guess would be a South American country like Brazil, Argentina, or even Colombia.

The Jaguar pressed on the tip of the blade, forcing the weapon back into its sheath until a distinct snap indicated it was locked in place.

"How does that pigsticker work?" Espinosa casually inquired.

"There is a button under the lock. All it takes is a flick of the wrist to operate."

"Maybe I should pick one up," Espinosa said, grinning. "I see they can come in real handy."

The Jaguar arranged his sleeve over the weapon, then looked at the dealer. "You need not worry about the report I will make to Mr. Remón."

"That's the best news I've heard in days," Espinosa declared, and turned to his men. "And now let's arrange a little surprise for Maria Salvato and her man friend."

7

Bolan and Maria sat on the front steps of her brownstone and watched a group of boys play stickball in the street. Traffic was sparse, and most of the pedestrians seemed intent on reaching home quickly after a hard day at work. The sun dipped partly below the western horizon, and a faint, cool northwesterly breeze heralded the advent of evening.

The warrior wore snug jeans and a flannel shirt that threatened to burst its buttons if he exhaled too forcefully. He glanced at a potted plant beside him, then at a small girl three doors down who regarded him with an air of friendly curiosity.

"Will you try your friend again soon?" Maria queried.

"I should," Bolan answered. "I don't understand why he hasn't gotten back to me by now."

"You're welcome to stay the night."

"What would the neighbors think?"

"Who cares?"

Bolan saw the invitation in her eyes. Was she sincere, or was this simply part of her scheme to persuade him to help her? He had to admit he liked the idea, and the temptation was almost irresistible.

"Is your name really Mike Belasko?" she unexpectedly asked.

"Does it matter?"

"No, I suppose not. And I know I shouldn't pry, because then you might want to know about those clothes I lent you."

"Your personal life is none of my business," Bolan said, observing a flight of pigeons over the grimy rooftops on the other side of Filisola. Although his left arm still pained him considerably, his strength had returned. He knew he should try harder to track down Brognola, but he couldn't bring himself to make the effort. That rarest of conditions for someone in his profession, a sense of serenity, temporarily alleviated the strain of constant danger, and he savored the opportunity to relax and briefly enjoy living.

"So when will you leave?"

"When the sun goes down."

Maria frowned. "At least let me cook you some supper."

"You've already fed me twice today."

"I don't mind." She placed her hand on his arm. "Wait here while I whip something up."

The warrior watched her to go inside. Maria was a decent, hardworking woman who deserved better than the tragedy Fate had dished out.

A black sedan cruised down the street, interrupting the stickball game and forcing the players to move to the sidewalks. It drove slowly to the end of the block, its tinted windows concealing the occupants, and took a right.

Bolan rose, watching the sedan disappear, a warning siren shrieking in his mind. He quickly went inside, walked to a closet near the kitchen where Maria had stashed his gear and opened it. Everything was piled on the floor. He squatted and picked up his blacksuit. Both the shirt and the pants were caked with grime, and the bottom half of the shirt was now stiff from the dried blood that had soaked into the fabric.

He deposited the clothes in a corner and reclaimed the Beretta and the Desert Eagle. Knowing the shoulder holster wouldn't fit under the tight flannel shirt, he opted to slip the Beretta under the garment at the small of his back, wedging the barrel under the top of the waistband. The Desert Eagle went into the waistband at the front of the pants. By letting the shirttails dangle, he effectively hid both weapons. Spare ammo went into his back pockets.

Next Bolan retrieved his Ka-bar fighting knife, which he secured to his right leg, just above the ankle. He removed a garrote from a slit pocket of the blacksuit, which he crammed into his right front pocket. The fragmentation grenades were inviting, but he left them there. If he was right, and if the battle reached the street, one of those grenades might take out any innocent bystanders who were in the vicinity. He straightened, closed the door and moved into the kitchen. "Got a question for you."

Maria was in the act of shaping ground beef into hamburger patties. She glanced at him, all smiles. "What is it?"

"Did you tell Hector Caro your address?"

"Of course not. Do you think I'm crazy?"

"No crazier than the rest of us. Is there any chance he could have followed you home?"

Maria paused and regarded him quizzically. "I guess so, but I didn't notice anyone trailing me after our two meetings. Why do you ask?"

"You met with him twice?"

"Yes. Once to set up the deal, and the second time to give him the money and receive the information I wanted."

"So he could have shadowed you back either time," Bolan said, staring out the window at the gradually darkening sky. Twilight would persist for an hour or more, which gave him a little time if the opposition was professional. They'd wait until dark to increase their advantage.

"Why? What's going on?"

"I saw a car go by out front."

"So? Lots of cars go by every day."

"I didn't like the looks of it," Bolan elaborated.

"Did you see someone inside who looked suspicious?"

"The windows were tinted."

"And you automatically assume there will be trouble?" Maria asked. "Has anyone ever told you that you're paranoid?"

"I'm cautious. There's a difference."

"If you say so," Maria said, chuckling as she resumed making their meal. "I hope you don't mind hamburgers. Tacos were my first choice, but I'm out of the shells."

"No problem. I'll be back in a bit." He returned to the stoop and scanned Filisola. The stickball game was just breaking up, and there was no sign of the sedan. He noticed the little girl in the same spot and gave her a friendly wave.

The child covered her mouth with her hand, giggled and waved, and ran into her house.

He went in again, locked the door behind him and ventured upstairs. There were two bedrooms, a bath and another closet. Both bedrooms, one at the front of the house and one at the rear, contained windows that couldn't be reached except by a ladder. He discounted the second floor as a means of entry for the attackers, and walked to the kitchen.

"The food will be ready in ten minutes," Maria announced, standing at the stove.

Bolan moved over to her side. "Why don't we eat out instead?"

"Don't be ridiculous. I know what you're trying to do."

"Oh?"

"You're trying to get me out of the house because of that car you saw. You think I'm in danger."

"You could be."

"You're making a mountain out of a molehill," Maria told him good-naturedly. "Espinosa isn't about to hit me in my own home. We're in the middle of the city, there are neighbors all around and the nearest police station is only eight blocks away.''

"If Slick Tony discovers you were at his estate, he'll hit you no matter where you are," Bolan said over his shoulder.

"How would he find out?"

"Caro."

"No way. Caro knows Espinosa will kill him if the truth came out. He'll steer clear of Slick Tony."

"You hope."

"Why must you always be so cynical?"

"Maria, when you've been in this business as long as I have, you know to never take anyone or anything for granted. Caro is a loose end, and loose ends always cause trouble."

"I wish I knew what 'business' you're in. You seem to know all about men like Espinosa and the way they do business. I also get the impression you've known much violence in your lifetime." She paused. "Who is April Rose?"

Bolan swung around in surprise. "How do you know about her?"

The big man's intensity caused Maria to recoil in alarm. "From you," she blurted. "You spoke her name when you were unconscious."

"What else did I say?" Bolan tried to resist the flood of bittersweet memories that the mere mention of April's name provoked. A vision of her lovely face seemed to hover in front of him, her luminous eyes conveying all the love in the world. Romanticists liked to talk about that "perfect someone" every person was destined to meet sooner or later. April Rose had been Bolan's.

"A few things," Maria said nervously.

"Like what?"

"You spoke the name Johnny twice, and once you mumbled a lot and I caught the name Hal."

"That was all?"

"There was one comment I didn't understand. Something about a stony man. You didn't say anything that gave me a clue to your true identity, if that's what you're worried about."

Bolan relaxed. He closed and locked the back door, then sat at the table, acutely conscious of her probing gaze following him every step of the way. "I'm sorry if I frightened you."

"Care to talk about it?"

"No."

"Okay."

Bolan saw the hurt in her eyes. "April Rose is dead. She—"

"There's no need to explain," Maria cut him off brusquely. "We've already agreed not to pry into each other's personal lives. Your past is your business. I'm only sorry I upset you so terribly." She turned to the stove.

Bolan rose and moved behind her. He hesitated, then gently placed his hands on her shoulders. "Don't blame yourself," he said softly. "I shouldn't have snapped at you. April is a part of my life I try not to think about."

Maria faced him, a trace of moisture in her eyes. "I know what you mean," she assured him, and impulsively leaned forward to lightly kiss him on the lips.

"What was that for?"

"Does there have to be a logical reason?" Maria replied. "Can't a woman and a man just let their feelings out?"

"It would never work."

"I don't want a lifelong commitment."

The warrior idly stared at the window, noting it was getting dark faster than he'd anticipated.

"Is something wrong?"

"I was thinking of that car."

Maria shook her head and laughed. "Don't you ever relax?"

"I can't afford to."

"We're not machines. We all need a little break now and then. You especially. I've never met anyone so tense all the time, like at any minute you expect someone to pop out and try to kill you."

Bolan shrugged. "You never know."

"Why don't we eat supper? Then I'll teach you how to really relax," Maria suggested, and added with a hint of apprehension, "unless, of course, you're still bound and determined to leave as soon as you can."

"I've changed my mind about leaving."

"I was hoping you'd say that," Maria stated, genuinely pleased. "Now don't molest me again or I'll end up burning our meal." She smiled and devoted her attention to the hamburgers.

Bolan relaxed and moved to the table. Perhaps she was right, he reflected. Maybe he was worried over nothing.

Maria picked up a towel and wiped her hands as she stepped to the light switch. "Let's brighten up this place," she proposed, reaching out her right hand.

At that instant, from the rear of the property came a loud crash.

8

Bolan reached Maria in two steps, pushing her hand away from the switch. "Don't," he ordered, pulling her to one side, behind the refrigerator.

"What's gotten into you? That was probably just a dog knocking over a trash can in the alley. Happens all the time."

"I'll check." Bolan went to the door, cautiously parted the green curtains and peered through the glass pane.

There were three of them, all armed, moving toward the house. The gunner in the middle limped. Evidently he was the one who had slipped while scaling the fence and knocked over a garbage can.

"We've got company," Bolan announced, drawing the Beretta and returning to Maria.

"I should have listened to you," Maria stated. "What do we do now?"

"Where's your gun?"

"Upstairs in the bedroom. Want me to go get it?"

"No," Bolan answered. "You stick with me." He glanced toward the hallway, wishing he had more room to maneuver. If there were hardmen out front, which there most likely were, the house was effectively sealed off. "They'll want to get in and get right out again before your neighbors notice anything unusual and call the police," he explained. "Time is on our side. If we can hold them off for a few minutes, they'll haul ass."

"Shouldn't we be calling the cops ourselves?"

Before Bolan could respond, the back door shook violently as someone outside slammed into it and twisted the knob. Bolan raised the Beretta, aimed at the center of the curtain and stroked the trigger twice. Glass shattered, and a cry of pain announced a hit.

Heartbeats later a hail of lead bored through the door, reducing the remainder of the glass to shards and splintering the wood in the bottom panel.

The warrior recognized the distinctive metallic chatter of Uzis. Since the refrigerator was to the left of the door, none of the rounds came close. But the kitchen table and chairs were blasted to pieces, wood slivers and chips flying in all directions.

Maria gasped and touched his arm.

Bolan waited until the firing ceased, then grabbed her hand and raced toward the hallway. The gaps in the door revealed two figures partly visible on the concrete steps. To discourage them he fired two shots in their direction and was gratified to see one of the men topple over. Hauling Maria after him, he dashed into the corridor.

A resounding crash came from the front door, but it held.

"We're boxed in!" Maria exclaimed.

The warrior halted and let go of her. He transferred the Beretta to his left hand, drew the Desert Eagle and flattened against the left-hand wall. From where he stood, he could see both doors.

Maria dived for the telephone and grabbed the handset. She frantically attempted to dial a number, scowled and slammed it down again. "It's dead!"

Out front a gruff voice barked, "Get back! It's set!"

The significance of the remark galvanized Bolan into action. There was no time to reach the stairs, which were ten feet closer to the entrance, so he whirled, looped his left arm around Maria's slim waist, and hurtled into the kitchen, bearing them both to the tile floor.

None too soon.

A huge explosion rocked the brownstone on its foundation, and smoke, dust and debris billowed down the hallway.

Bolan took advantage of the swirling, acrid cloud. For all of thirty seconds the gunners on the stoop wouldn't be able to see a thing inside, and they'd wait until the cloud dispersed. He had that long to make his play.

A hardman abruptly barreled through the back door, splitting the remaining wood with kicks and his elbows. Framed in the doorway, he spied the pair on the floor and tried to bring his Uzi into play.

Bolan got off two shots from his prone position, the big .44 booming and bucking.

As if an invisible sledgehammer had nailed him in the chest, the hardman was blown off his feet and out the door.

"Move!" Bolan ordered, as he got to his feet, Maria at his side. He ran to the doorway, paused to confirm there were three bodies lying sprawled in the yard and exited the house.

"Where are we going?" Maria asked anxiously.

"Just stay close." Bolan stuck both guns under his belt and stooped to retrieve a fallen Uzi. A rapid check verified it held a full magazine. He sprinted to the back fence, seeking a way out, and spied a narrow closed gate in the southeast corner. They were there in seconds, only to discover a sturdy combination lock thwarted his intent.

"I'll open it," Maria offered.

"No time," Bolan told her. "We'll go over." He slipped behind her and gripped her under the arms.

"What are you doing?"

"This," Bolan stated, and heaved.

Maria raised her arms, grasping the top of the fence, clinging in desperation as she struggled to pull herself up.

"Here," Bolan said, taking hold of her legs and pushing. The added impetus was all that was needed to carry her to the far side, and the warrior pivoted before making his own escape to check for pursuit.

A lone gunner emerged, his gaze fixed on the three bodies instead of sweeping the yard.

The warrior let the Uzi point out the man's mistake, and even as the gunner crumpled to the ground he whirled and vaulted upward. His left arm painfully protested the strain when he hooked his elbow on the top of the fence.

"They're out here!" someone shouted.

Bolan dropped on the other side. He landed lightly, the Uzi in his left hand, and immediately took off to the north.

Maria fell into step beside him. "Where to now?"

"Do you have the keys to your van?"

"In my pocket."

"Then we get the hell out of here."

They raced to the end of the alley and halted. The big man peered into the street, saw nothing amiss and led the way to Filisola while holding the Uzi low and behind his left leg so as not to terrify the few pedestrians they passed. He slowed at the intersection and cautiously looked toward her house.

The black sedan was parked at the curb two doors down from the brownstone. Thirty feet to the north, closer to them, was the van. Filisola appeared deserted. The front door to Maria's house had been blown to bits, and many of the windows on both sides of the streets were shattered.

"We have to move quickly." Bolan walked casually into the open, pretending he was about to cross the intersection. He stepped past the first parked car, then cut sharply to the left, heading for her brown van.

A siren wailed off in the distance.

Bolan wasn't about to wait for the police. He'd wind up in custody so fast it would make his head swim. His best bet was to reach Brognola and let the big Fed handle the legal ramifications.

"What's going on out here, mister?"

The warrior turned at the sound of the angry voice. A bald man stood on the steps of a house across the street, his hands on his hips. Bolan ignored him and kept running.

"Did you hear me?" the irate citizen demanded louder.

"He'll give us away," Maria said.

Bolan shared her concern. He straightened and risked glancing at the brownstone. As yet, none of the opposition was in sight. All the hardmen were either inside or belatedly trailing them out the alley. A glance over his shoulder assured him they were still safe in that respect.

The bald man wasn't done with them. "I'll have you know I called the cops!" he yelled.

"Estupido," Maria muttered.

They drew within one car length of the van, when suddenly five gunners burst from the brownstone and hurried to the sedan.

Bolan grabbed Maria and ducked into the space between her vehicle and the car in front. He crouched and listened to the sedan's engine being revved. Seconds later the car streaked past and took a left at the intersection.

The sound of sirens grew rapidly louder.

"I'll drive," Bolan volunteered, stepping to the door and sliding in behind the wheel.

Maria climbed in the other side and gave him the keys. "Follow those sons of bitches," she suggested angrily.

Bolan was inclined to do just that, but the thought of exposing her to further danger deterred him. So far they'd been lucky, and luck had a way of running out when it was least expected. He placed the Uzi in his lap, started the van and pulled out, turning on the headlights.

An earsplitting explosion unexpectedly rocked the entire neighborhood, totally destroying the brownstone. Tongues of vivid flame shot from the front, and a cloud of fire and debris billowed skyward. Windows in the nearby buildings that remained undamaged by the previous blast were shattered to pieces.

The warrior clutched the steering wheel firmly as a wall of concussive force slammed into the rear of the vehicle and propelled it sideways. A parked station wagon materialized in its path and he spun the wheel hard left to avert a collision. The front fender came within a hairbreadth of smashing into the wagon's side, and then he was in the clear and in control. He took the left turn sharply, the tires squealing.

A block and a half ahead, cruising at the speed limit to avoid arousing suspicion, was the sedan.

"There they are!" Maria shouted.

Bolan simply nodded. Here was a golden opportunity to discover Espinosa's whereabouts. All he had to do was shadow the hardmen. The risks were minimal if he hung back far enough to permit a quick getaway should the gunners make the van. So although having the woman along bothered him, he decided to go for it.

"Whatever you do, don't lose them," Maria urged, leaning forward.

The warrior glanced at her. "You don't seem very broken up about your house."

Maria blinked, then gave a little shrug. "Sure I am. But now isn't the time to get upset about the loss." She gripped the dashboard, her face flushed from the excitement. "Besides, what's a house compared to the possibility of nailing Slick Tony?"

Bolan frowned. He began to suspect that her quest for vengeance was more like an obsession. Otherwise, how could she take the loss of everything she owned so casually. "Do you realize that some of your neighbors could be lying dead or injured back there?"

Without batting a lash, Maria responded, "The police and the ambulance crews will take care of them."

As if on cue, a police car appeared ahead. The shriek of its siren and the flashing of its twin cherry rotating beacons served to clear a path down the middle of the street as all other vehicles moved dutifully aside.

Bolan did likewise, hugging the right-hand curb until the patrol car went past. He resumed the chase, his eyes glued to the sedan. Something gnawed at the back of his mind, something other than his concern for Maria Slavato. It wasn't until he happened to glance in the rearview mirror and spotted a dark blue sedan with tinted windows that he knew the reason.

The numbers had been all wrong.

He'd disposed of four gunners and seen five more leave the house, for a grand total of nine. It was highly unlikely they all arrived in a single car. There had to have been two vehicles, and now he was stuck between them. Those in the blue sedan were bound to notice the van eventually, if they hadn't already.

"If we do find Espinosa, I hope you'll let me take care of him," Maria said.

"Have you ever killed anyone?" Bolan inquired absently, pondering the best move to make. Any quick maneuvers would draw unwanted attention.

"No. But that doesn't mean I can't."

"If you do, you'll never be the same person. Killing changes you, Maria, and not always for the better."

Bolan spied a supermarket parking lot a hundred feet in front of them, on the left side of the street. All he had to do was whip in there, wait for the blue sedan to go by, then follow both cars.

"Espinosa is the only one I've ever wanted to kill, except for my former husband, of course," Maria stated. "It's not as if I'll become a coldhearted murderer by doing the world a favor and disposing of a rotten drug lord."

The warrior flipped on the turn signal and braked.

"What are you doing?" Maria asked.

"Playing it safe. There might be more of Espinosa's men behind us."

"How do you know?"

"Call it an educated guess."

"But what if you're wrong?"

Bolan spun the wheel and entered the parking lot. "Don't worry. We won't lose them."

"You hope."

The warrior looked into the rearview mirror again, expecting to see the second sedan heading westward. Instead, to his surprise, he saw it following the van. A quick glance at the far end of the lot disclosed another ominous fact. The black sedan had doubled back and was just pulling into another entrance farther down.

Maria observed the big man's features harden. "What's wrong?"

"They've made us," Bolan said. "Hang on to your seat."

9

"How did they figure out who we are?" Maria asked.

"The men in the second car probably saw us pull out and follow their buddies," Bolan speculated. He drove down an aisle and braked.

The sedans had slowed to a snail's pace.

"Let's make a break for it," Maria proposed.

"With all these innocent bystanders around?" Bolan replied, indicating the packed lot with a jerk of his hand. "Not on your life."

"We can't just stay here."

True, Bolan thought, wondering if the hardmen were foolish enough to engage him in such a public spot. Since the police were already swarming the area, any new disturbance would draw the boys in blue in droves.

"Why don't we park this thing and try to lose them on foot?"

"They'd catch us in no time," Bolan said. He didn't bother to add that a running firefight on a crowded Miami street was to be avoided at all costs. Each sedan had stopped and was idling near one of the exits.

The only way out of the parking lot was past the gunners.

"How did the guys in the first car know to turn around?"

"Car phones in both vehicles would be my guess."

The warrior turned left down a different aisle and drove slowly toward the east boundary. Beyond lay a side street, with a low hedge separating the sparse traffic from the lot. "Is your van insured?" he casually inquired.

"Yes. But what does my insurance have to do with anything?"

"Just in case."

"In case what?"

"That hedge is harder than it looks," Bolan stated, and floored the accelerator. The van surged forward, the engine growling. He angled toward the southeast corner, alert for any pedestrians, hoping to reach the street before the gunners clued in to his strategy. If he could lose them, he'd find a place to hole up until he contacted Brognola. A glance in the mirror disclosed his strategy hadn't been entirely successful.

Already the sedans were speeding recklessly in pursuit, their horns blaring as they skirted shoppers and other vehicles.

So much for the idea that Espinosa's men would prefer a low profile, Bolan reflected wryly. They seemed intent on eliminating Maria and him no matter what it took. Perhaps Slick Tony had put a price on their heads, a price high enough to justify the taking of any risks. He tightened his grip and concentrated on making good their escape.

The van plowed into the hedge doing fifty miles an hour, emerging unscathed. Bolan took a sharp right, lurching in his seat, and sped to the next junction where he took a left.

"I don't see them yet," Maria announced.

The big man hung a right at the first crossway, putting the pedal to the metal when he found a deserted stretch of asphalt ahead. He traveled six blocks before taking yet another left.

"Still no sign of them," Maria said. "I think we did it."

Bolan began to relax. The odds of being overtaken were slimmer by the second. Their surroundings had changed, the homes and businesses giving way to an industrial district. There were fewer streetlights and hardly any people on the sidewalks. He continued on for another minute, then spied an alley on the left and wheeled into it.

"What are you doing?" Maria asked as he parked.

"We need to talk."

"About what?"

"You."

"What about me?"

Bolan faced her. "The way you behaved back there, as if you don't care about anything except getting Espinosa."

"I don't. He's responsible for the death of my son. What would you have me do? Send him a thank-you card?"

"Be serious," Bolan stated. He leaned over and took her hand in his. "Maria, I know what you've been through. I've been there myself. But you've got to be careful you don't go overboard. If you let it, your craving for vengeance will ruin your life."

"It already has. I know you mean well, but I can never rest until I've paid Espinosa back. Never."

Bolan opened his mouth to try to convince her otherwise, when the roar of a car engine reverberated in the alley and the black sedan abruptly materialized behind them, blocking the mouth.

"They found us!" Maria exclaimed. "How?"

The warrior wondered the same thing as he threw the gearshift into Drive and headed for the opposite end of the alley. He barely got the speedometer over twenty before he had to stand on the brakes.

Driving into the other end was the second sedan.

"Give me a gun," Maria demanded.

Bolan ignored her, threw open his door, gripped the Uzi in his right hand and jumped out. "Come on," he commanded, glancing both ways. Gunners were spilling from the two vehicles.

The warrior turned. They were trapped between a pair of three-story structures, either manufacturing concerns or warehouses. Ten feet to his right was a wooden door, and he grabbed her hand and ran toward it.

"They're making a break!" someone bellowed.

Bolan hugged the wall as an Uzi cut loose with a sustained burst, the rounds smacking into the macadam within inches of his feet. He squeezed off a short burst to discourage the opposition and reached the door. A quick twist of the knob confirmed it was locked.

To their rear a silenced revolver coughed twice, the bullets thudding into the wall above their heads.

The warrior trained the Uzi on the wood adjacent to the knob and stitched a semicircular pattern of holes that shattered the wood. He didn't waste time with a kick; he simply rammed his left shoulder into the panel and felt the lock give way with a distinct crunch. The door swung open, and he found himself in a dimly lighted corridor.

Bolan pivoted. "Run," he told Maria, and the instant she dashed past him he risked a look outside. There were four hardmen to the left, five to the right who were closer. A tall gunner pointed a pistol and snapped off a shot that struck the jamb near Bolan's temple. Returning the favor, the warrior drilled the gunner in the chest, and as the tall man toppled, the rest dived for cover.

The tactic had bought Bolan twenty seconds, at most. He wheeled and sprinted after Maria. He glanced into the rooms lining the corridor, noting offices and rooms crammed high with stacked boxes.

Maria arrived at a junction and stopped to wait for him. "Which way?" she asked when the warrior reached her.

Identical hallways stretched in both directions, and he took the right branch for no specific reason. Maria stayed on his heels until they reached a closed door.

Bolan tried the knob, and this time fortune smiled on him. The door opened soundlessly to reveal an immense chamber that contained scores of rows of sewing machines mounted on long narrow tables bordered by chairs. Half a dozen irregularly spaced fluorescent lights cast a pale glow over everything.

"I hear them coming," Maria whispered urgently.

So did Bolan. The warrior motioned for her to precede him, then entered and closed the door. He moved among the tables, traveling a third of the way across the chamber before he squatted in the shadows.

"What are you doing?"

"You wanted a gun, didn't you?" Bolan reminded her, and reloaded his weapons. He gave the Beretta to her, while the Desert Eagle went back into his waistband. "Now let's find a way out of here," he proposed, and started to rise.

The door swung open with a crash and three hardmen darted across the threshold, crouched and fanned out. One held an Uzi, one an Ingram MAC-10 and the third a pistol-grip shotgun.

Bolan flattened and pulled Maria down. He peered through the forest of chair legs and detected movement at three points. One of the gunners was heading directly toward them. Taking Maria's hand again, he stealthily made for the opposite side, hoping to elude the trio and escape without another confrontation.

From somewhere up ahead a cold voice shattered the silence. "Ramon. Ted. Alfredo. They're between us and moving my way. Go slow. Drive them in this direction."

The warrior halted and scanned the far wall, attempting to spot the speaker. There were several open doors leading to darkened rooms or corridors, and he couldn't tell which one concealed his target. Somehow, the man seemed to know their exact location. He slanted to the right, keeping low, alert for threats from front and back.

"Why not give up now, Ms. Salvato, and save us both a lot of grief?" the speaker called out.

Bolan had to halt when Maria abruptly gasped and stopped.

"My men have this building sealed off, lady," the man went on. "There's no way you can get out in one piece. And if you're thinking of stalling until the cops show, think again. One of my men is monitoring a police scanner in the car, and he'll let me know the second they head in this direction. We'll be long gone before they arrive." The speaker paused. "And then we'll track you down and finish the job, only you'll suffer even more for all the aggravation you've caused me."

Tugging on Maria's arm, Bolan tried to get her moving again. But she was riveted to the spot, listening with bated breath, her behavior confirming what he'd always known. There was no place for amateurs in the death-dealing business. The greener a person was, the faster they died.

"What will it be, Ms. Salvato? I'm in a generous mood. Surrender now and I'll let you live. If you don't, I'll have you skinned alive."

Maria looked at Bolan. "What do we do?"

"We find a way out of here."

"But you heard him. We don't stand a prayer."

"That's what he'd like you to believe. Don't you see he's toying with you? We can make it if you don't give up."

Brittle laughter seemed to echo off the walls. "If you listen to your protector, Ms. Salvato, you'll be chopped into bits and fed to alligators. He knows it's hopeless. He's just trying to delay the inevitable."

The warrior stared at a murky doorway in the middle of the wall, certain the speaker was beyond it. Obviously the man overheard every word they uttered. How? His best guess was a sound detector, a top-of-the-line long-range microphone sporting a portable parabolic dish. If so, it explained the ease with which the gunners found them. A professional could use a sound detector to trail a vehicle, even in heavy traffic, by training his ear to selectively separate the distinctive audio signature of a given muffler from all other noises. And a two-mile range on such devices wasn't uncommon.

"Maybe we should do as he says," Maria suggested.

"Like hell." Bolan turned, prepared to drag her if need be, and saw the gunner carrying the Ingram pop into view at the end of the table on his right. Instinctively he gave the man a terminal case of lead poisoning, then hauled Maria after him as he broke into a run. If he kept on the go, the guy employing the electronic ear would have a difficult time pinpointing their position.

"Behind us!" Maria shouted.

The warrior glanced back to see the hardmen with the shotgun sliding across a table into their aisle. The warrior swung the Uzi around before the gunner could bring the shotgun to bear, and swept the subgun in a tight figure-eight pattern. The impacts flung the man onto his back.

Bolan began to pivot when he noticed Maria's eyes widen in alarm. She was gazing over his shoulder, and he could only assume the third hardman was taking a bead on him. She raised the Beretta and fired twice. The gunner went down, a new pair of holes in his face.

"Get them!" the phantom speaker roared. "But I want the woman alive!"

The Executioner discarded the Uzi as he dashed to the end of the row and drew the large silver Desert Eagle. More of Espinosa's men charged through the doors. He squatted and slid under the left-hand table, using the chairs as cover. It wasn't much, but it was the best he could do under the circumstances.

Maria crouched beside him and said ever so quietly, "I'm sorry for getting you into this mess."

Bolan wasn't about to argue the issue. He glimpsed gunners moving about the chamber on all sides. Without Maria along, he would have taken them head-on and given as good as he got. But his first priority was to get her out of there alive. He waited until there were no hardmen in the immediate vicinity, then slid out with her in tow. There was a door in the corner that might just be their ticket out.

"Why are you drawing this out?" demanded the man with the voice of ice. "The longer you do, the madder I'll get. And you don't want to get Tony Espinosa ticked off. Take my word for it."

So now Bolan had an identity. Any hood with brains would have left the operation to subordinates, but not Slick Tony. As the warrior well knew, Espinosa liked to take a personal hand in snuffing those who gave him trouble. It was stupid and careless, true, but at least Espinosa made certain the job got done right the first time.

The warrior and the woman stayed in the shadows and progressed another twenty-five yards.

Just as Bolan convinced himself that they had a good chance of making it, he heard the telltale scrape of a sole on the tile floor. Across the nearest table, his back to them, was a hefty gunner carrying an H&K-33. The big man straightened just high enough for his arm to clear the tabletop, and fired.

As if he were jet propelled, the hardman flew forward onto the next row of tables, his arms flung out, and landed on top of a sewing machine.

Bolan turned and managed a few quick strides, staying as low as before, skirting the end of a row. Out of the corner of his left eye he glimpsed a dark-clad form leaping at them and tried to shove Maria out of harm's way while simultaneously diving to the floor. A flying foot caught him in the shoulder and sent him tumbling into the wall, and although he recovered instantly and rose on one knee he was already too late.

A man wearing a loose black suit had his left arm clamped around Maria's slim throat. In his right hand, and seeming to extend from under his sleeve, was a long slender blade, its point almost touching Maria's eye. "Even if you get me, she will lose the eye," he said quickly.

Bolan almost shot anyway. But the man in black was using Maria as a shield, exposing just his arms and the right side of his face. A snap shot might do the trick, yet at what cost to her? Reluctantly he let the Desert Eagle's barrel drop.

Instead of smirking or gloating, the innately menacing figure nodded. "I expected as much. You are a man of honor, like myself."

"I don't know what you're talking about," Bolan said, conscious of hardmen converging from all directions.

"We are both in the same profession, I think."

Despite the situation, Bolan was intrigued. The guy could have wasted him, but didn't. Why not?

"Do you remember me?"

Suddenly the Executioner did. "We met the other night. You almost nailed me."

A smile twisted the man's lips. "And you gave me a scar I will bear to my grave."

The hardmen arrived, five of them training their weapons on the warrior and nervously eyeing the Desert Eagle.

"I would put that down if I were you," the man in black suggested. "These men lack our self-control, and you know how dangerous a nervous finger can be."

Bolan slowly deposited the .44 on the floor and elevated his hands. If surrender meant a few more minutes of precious life, he'd play along in the hope of turning the tide.

"You are a wise man," the man in black said in a sincere tone. "And one of the best I have ever seen. An equal, in fact." His voice sounded wistful. "I have met so few who deserved such a distinction."

A newcomer abruptly entered the conversation. "What the hell is going on here?"

Bolan glanced around and recognized the angular features of a face he'd seen only in a file Brognola had shown him. Antonio Espinosa in person. Behind the drug lord walked a gunner and a man holding a parabolic mike.

"I thought I gave orders to kill this son of a bitch," Espinosa snapped, jabbing a finger at the warrior. "Why is he still alive?"

The man in black released Maria and turned to Espinosa. "The fault is mine. I wanted to repay you for allowing me to dispose of your problem earlier." He paused. "I thought you might like to take care of him personally."

Espinosa grinned. "I didn't figure you for the sentimental type. But you're right. If there's one thing I've learned in this world, it's to never let anyone else wash your own dirty laundry." He swiveled to give the prisoner the benefit of a baleful stare. "Got any last prayers, sucker?"

10

The Executioner gauged the span between them and tensed to spring. If nothing else, he'd take Espinosa out with him. He was ready to uncurl when he heard the patter of running feet, and a man burst through the middle doorway, shouting in a panic.

"Tony! Tony!"

At the cry all eyes, with the exception of those of the man in black, swung toward the late arrival.

"What the hell is it, Nick?" Espinosa demanded.

"The cops—" Nick began, and stopped when the howl of approaching sirens punctuated his message.

Even the man with the blade cocked his head to listen.

Bolan made his move, coming off the floor in a rush, his right hand scooping up the Desert Eagle, his legs pumping as he ran to the closest table and vaulted up and over it. Behind him a pistol belatedly barked, the slugs thudding into the tabletop under him. He arced down onto his right shoulder and rolled, smashing into the next line of folding metal chairs and bowling several over. In one fluid motion he surged under the table and crawled out the far side.

There was a method to the big man's madness. Since he couldn't take on all those hardmen at once *and* protect Maria, he planned to draw them away so he could dispose of them without fear of her being caught in the cross fire. Then he'd effect her rescue. With the police on the way, the gunners would be eager to terminate him quickly, and might become careless. He rose high enough to see over the tables, expecting to find Espinosa's hardmen in frantic pursuit. Instead, to his surprise, they were all simply standing there and smirking as if at a private joke. He brought up the .44 hoping to bag Espinosa, when the drug lord suddenly dropped from view and shouted a single word.

"Now!"

An instant of bafflement gave way to stark comprehension when Bolan saw the circular metallic object sail in his direction. He whirled and leaped onto the last row of tables, keenly conscious as he jumped to the floor that he had mere seconds to get out of the kill radius. The doorway ahead beckoned with the promise of partial shelter, and he ran all out, counting down in his mind.

Three.

The warrior was still four feet from the door when he launched himself into the air, his arms outstretched.

Two.

Bolan cleared the jamb, jerking to the left in midair, glimpsing the vague outline of a desk below him. He whipped downward like a diver knifing off a high dive, but his fingers were still inches from the floor when the detonation took place. The confines of the office amplified the explosion, the thundering blast causing torturous pain in his ears even as the concussion from the grenade caught his legs and buffeted him as if he were a leaf in a whirlwind. He tumbled head over heels and slammed into a nearby wall. The crash jarred him to his core and he came down hard on his head and shoulders, stunned, a millisecond before the desk and other furniture smashed into his bruised body. The world went black, then he drifted in and out of consciousness.

Somewhere, someone screamed; there were shouts and shots.

The warrior felt sensation return and struggled to collect his thoughts. He shook his head vigorously, then stopped, racked with an intense spasm. Gritting his teeth, he took stock and discovered he was upside down, wedged between what was left of the desk and the wall. His ears were ringing, his eyes watering. Through it all he had managed to hold on to the .44.

Bolan shoved on the desk and swung his feet down, rising too rapidly. Dizziness engulfed him, and he leaned on the wall for support. A clammy substance trickled from his right ear, and he didn't need to touch it to know he was bleeding. After a few seconds he pushed through the debris toward the doorway, which was now twice as wide thanks to the grenade. The ringing in his ears interfered with his hearing, and he couldn't be sure but he thought he heard gunshots in the distance. Concerned for Maria's safety, he stepped to the jagged opening.

Espinosa and his gunners were gone. So was the guy
in black. And so was Maria Salvato.

Bolan emerged from the demolished office and
turned to the right, making for the doorway through
which Espinosa had appeared, gathering strength with
each stride. He inhaled deeply, thinking of how he'd
failed Maria when she'd needed him the most. At the
door he paused to squat and search the floor, double-
checking, but there was no sign of her body or blood.
A certain measure of relief consoled him as he hurried down another corridor. The caress of a cool
breeze on his face confirmed the passage led to an exit,
and he increased his speed.

There was so much to do.

Contact Brognola.

Get patched up.

And, if it was the last thing he ever did, find Maria
and eliminate Antonio Espinosa.

"Striker, you look like hell."

Bolan glanced at Hal Brognola. "Thanks. I needed
that."

The Executioner and the Justice man were in room
118 at the Flamingo Hotel, just off Interstate 95. A
tourist trap in every sense of the word, the decorator
responsible for the color scheme had simplified the
task by having everything painted in bright, shocking
pink: the walls, the ceiling, the floor, even the furniture. To complement the assault on good taste, a large
plastic flamingo was attached to the wall above the

bed's headboard. Naturally the long-legged bird was pink.

"Maybe I should call that doctor back and have you reexamined," Brognola commented. "I don't think he earned his pay."

"That's two for two," Bolan said, reaching up to touch his right ear. The painkillers the doctor provided had done wonders. "Why don't we get down to cases."

"Fine by me," Brognola responded, intently studying the warrior. "If you think you're up to it."

"I am."

"Fair enough. First off, let me apologize for the crossed signals. When we discovered Espinosa had flown the coop, I sent in Leo with a team of specialists to go over the estate. To tell you the truth, I half expected to find you lying in the dirt out there. I'm glad I didn't."

Bolan noted the frank sincerity in his friend's voice.

"I'm afraid your message was misplaced in the shuffle. When the secretary at Justice finally got the word to me, I tried to call you. I kept getting a recording saying there were network difficulties, so I had Leo go over to check out the address." Brognola paused. "You can imagine my surprise when he phoned and told me the house had been blown all to hell and the police had the whole block cordoned off."

Bolan remained silent.

"The next thing I know, the media is reporting there's some kind of gang war going on over drugs. The police respond to a strange incident at a supermarket where someone plows right through a hedge, and then they receive word that shots have been fired at a clothing manufacturer's. They investigated and wound up tangling with Espinosa's crew. Lost an officer in the gun battle."

"But Espinosa got away."

"I'm afraid so. The cops got two of his men, though."

"Terrific."

The caustic comment concerned Brognola. "What's bothering you, Striker."

"Do you have an hour to kill?"

"I'm all yours."

"Then let me explain," Bolan offered, and did so, sticking to the pertinent facts, detailing his involvement with Maria, his confrontation with Espinosa and his two encounters with the man in black. To conclude, he said, "Just so you know, I'm going after her."

"I'll do what I can to help. There are a few facts you're not aware of, though. The scenario has changed drastically, Striker, for the worse."

"How do you mean?"

The big Fed filled him in on the recently discovered link between Espinosa and Harmodio Remón. He also related what little was known about Remón's top man. "From the description you've given me, I'd say the guy with the blade was the Jaguar. It conclusively proves the intel I received."

"This Jaguar was awful high on himself. He seemed to think we share some common bond because we're both professionals. Even treated me with a certain bizarre courtesy,'' Bolan disclosed.

"Don't let his behavior fool you. He really is one of the top ten in the business, and he deserves his rep. If you two meet again, he probably won't be so courteous."

"Do you have any leads on Espinosa's current location?"

"I wish. Every available agent is working on the case, but so far we have zip."

"Damn."

"Don't give up hope yet. There's one piece of information that may pan out. I had a phone call about eight hours ago from my friend at the DEA. It seems his people believe they have deciphered the fourth word their agent wrote on the wall as he died. The word was Trinity, and they think it stands for Trinity Island."

"Part of the Keys?" Bolan asked, referring to the string of islands and reefs that stretched about two hundred miles from southern Florida into the Gulf of Mexico. Drug runners and other smugglers used the Keys as entry points into the U.S.

"No," Brognola replied. "Trinity Island is one of the Ten Thousand Islands, as they're called, located off the southwest coast of the state. Most are situated between Cape Romano and Chokoloskee. They're isolated and, for the most part, sparsely populated. Trinity Island is an ideal spot to use for bringing in large drug shipments."

"What's being done about it?"

"The DEA has posted a surveillance team there in the hope of making a big score soon. If you want, I can call my friend Keating and volunteer your services in the spirit of interdepartmental cooperation." Brognola paused and smiled. "I expect they'll be happy to have the assistance since they're chronically understaffed."

Bolan pondered the offer. He preferred to work alone, but Trinity Island was the only link to Espinosa's organization and might well be his only hope of learning Maria's fate. There was one other possibility, however. "You mentioned an informer who supplied Carter with information. What are the chances of learning this informer's identity so I can pay him a visit?"

"I already know his name."

"You do?"

"Yep. It's Fernando Rascel."

"Why didn't you mention this sooner?" Bolan asked. "Do you know where he can be found?"

"In the morgue. The coast guard found a floater in Biscayne Bay yesterday, and it turned out to be Rascel. Evidently Espinosa found out or suspected him of spilling the beans."

So much for that idea, Bolan reflected. If he wanted to track down Maria, he had to go to Trinity Island. "About working with the DEA. What sort of cover are you thinking of?"

"You'll go as Mike Belasko, our veteran troubleshooter. Shouldn't raise any eyebrows that way."

"Sounds okay."

"Just don't get carried away."

"I wouldn't think of it."

11

Trinity Island would make an ideal snake sanctuary, Bolan decided after two days of fruitless waiting. He was concealed in dense vegetation to the south of a long, narrow field. The temperature hovered above ninety, and the humidity was close to one hundred percent. Just lying still, he sweated from every pore. Thankfully his camouflage fatigues were baggy enough to permit some ventilation.

The warrior once again wore a Beretta in a shoulder holster and packed the big Desert Eagle on his right hip. Military webbing and pouches held the ammo and other accessories he needed. Instead of an M-16, he held a gun that qualified as one of his favorites, a Weatherby Mark V Safari Grade big game rifle. When it came to picking off single targets at a distance, he preferred the bolt-action Mark V over all others. Superbly crafted, almost elegant in design, it was also one of the most reliably accurate guns he'd ever used.

Lying in the grass near his right forearm was the green walkie-talkie that served as his link to the four DEA agents who were scattered around the field. One of them was Brognola's friend, Bill Keating, a straight-arrow sort of guy Bolan had taken an immediate liking to when they were introduced. He'd seen the question mark in Keating's eyes, but the agent hadn't pried.

The three other agents were named Williams, Kuykendall and Seavers, who just might pose a problem. The youngest of the bunch, Seavers had impressed Bolan as being cocky and impetuous, a firebrand determined to strut his stuff and eager to move up in the agency. Seavers was the one Bolan would have to keep an eye on when and if anything happened.

Brognola had been right. Lying there and surveying the terrain, Bolan could readily understand why Espinosa, or whoever, had picked Trinity Island. Located at the westernmost fringe of the Ten Thousand Islands and well out into the Gulf of Mexico, the island offered certain advantages a drug runner would find irresistible. It was remote, it was easily accessible from the sea and a ring of tangled growth formed a protective wall around the field in the middle, shielding the landing site from the curious eyes of any boaters.

But there was still the possibility the DEA boys had misinterpreted Carter's cryptic message, or that whatever the informant had told Carter would go down on the island had already transpired. In which case Bolan was wasting his time.

The radio crackled to life. "Mike, are you awake?" Bill Keating asked.

"Affirmative."

"It's getting close to four p.m. If I send the signal to my men in Naples, the boat can be here in an hour to pick us up. I want your opinion on whether we go or stay."

"You're thinking of calling it quits?"

"Affirmative. We've been here forty-eight hours already, and I'm beginning to wonder if another twenty-four will even make a difference. We haven't seen hide nor hair of anyone, and from the looks of the grass in that field, a plane hasn't landed here in weeks, maybe months. There are no tire tracks, nothing." Keating paused. "Hal told me you're keen on nailing Espinosa, so I know this might be a disappointment. I want the bastard, too. But we both might do better trying other avenues. What do you say?"

Bolan hesitated. He'd entertained similar thoughts, but he was still reluctant to give up on the only true lead they had. "How about if we wait until dark? Another four or five hours won't make that much of a difference."

"Not to us, but Seavers is grousing because we ran out of canned peaches last night," Keating said, and static hissed for a few seconds. "All right. I agree. We might as well stick it out until the end of the day. After we get back, I'll contact the coast guard and have them keep an eye on this island. Not that it will do much good."

Bolan knew what the man meant. Try as they might, the coast guard couldn't be everywhere at once, and their regular patrols could be easily avoided by smugglers who could afford state-of-the-art detection equipment. High-tech radar alone enabled the bad guys to spot coast guard vessels miles off and initiate evasive maneuvers. Since Espinosa had already demonstrated a taste for a technological edge, as with the helicopter and the parabolic microphone, it was unlikely he'd simply waltz in without taking adequate security precautions.

The warrior settled in for the wait, listening to the buzz of countless insects and the chirping of birds. He thought of Maria and envisioned her floating somewhere in the Everglades, then shook his head to dispel the morbid thought.

Bolan was tired of seeing friends die for the cause. He'd lost family members, the woman he loved, close friends and fellow soldiers since he'd started his war everlasting, and through it all he'd stoically accepted the losses as inevitable. But every man had his limits, and Bolan never wanted to lose another person he cared for. He knew he wasn't being realistic, knew his emotions were getting the better of him, yet he didn't resist. He couldn't help how he felt, and if he tried to suppress his feelings he'd wind up being no better than the cold killers he fought.

The afternoon dragged on. The Executioner stayed alert, relying on the superb self-discipline he'd honed to perfection in the jungles of Southeast Asia. He listened for any break, however faint, in the pattern of the natural order. The sun headed for the western horizon, and once it set, so would his hopes.

A six o'clock the faint whine of a high-performance engine wafted over the island.

The warrior stiffened, his nerves tingling as the sound grew louder and louder. A speedboat, he speculated, moving in from the west. It could be a vacationer or a fisherman, but intuitively he knew it wasn't.

Steadily increasing in volume, the whine became a roar that sent startled seabirds on the western side of the island soaring skyward.

Bolan saw the gulls flapping upward, a sure sign the speedboat must be putting in to the sliver of beach. His radio crackled again.

"We've got company," Keating said.

At last, Bolan thought. He slid to a nearby tree, taking the radio along, and rose to his knees, then focused on the vegetation bordering the west edge of the field. He didn't have long to wait before figures appeared in the trees, eight in all.

Two gunners armed with M-1 carbines were in the lead. Then came the big man himself, Antonio Espinosa, wearing an immaculate white suit. Behind him was the man known as the Jaguar, dressed in black as usual.

Bolan took one look at the fifth person in line and felt his pulse quicken.

Maria Salvato looked the worse for wear. Her clothes were rumpled, her features downcast, her shoulders slumped as she walked. She stared at the ground, her arms hardly moving.

Trailing her were three hardmen. Two held MAC-10 submachine guns suspended from their shoulders by web straps. The last man had a backpack perched on his shoulders.

The warrior pressed his right eye to the telescopic sight on the Weatherby and adjusted it until he could count the bruises on Maria's face. And there were a lot of them. Her left eye was swollen almost shut, her lips puffy. She briefly gazed straight ahead, and his eyes narrowed as he noted her rigid, almost lifeless expression.

Moving quickly, Espinosa and his party hiked twenty yards into the field, then halted. He and the Jaguar conversed, then the drug lord gestured at the man with the backpack.

Bolan watched as the last man in line walked forward, removed the backpack and knelt. Unfastening the top flap, the man exposed a radio that he promptly proceeded to operate. The warrior wondered who the man was contacting. Maybe a big shipment was coming in. If so, why was the Jaguar present? To observe how smoothly Espinosa's operation worked? Or could it be something else, something bigger?

Subtle movement registered to the east.

The big man looked and frowned. He recognized the lanky form of Agent Seavers creeping toward the field's boundary. If the man wasn't careful, he'd give the operation away. He saw Seavers go to the ground behind a trunk and breathed a sigh of relief.

Espinosa and company were moving toward the north end, the gunners in a protective ring around their boss, who suddenly stepped close to Maria and draped his arm around her shoulder. He made a comment that provoked laughter from his henchmen.

Of all those in the party, only the Jaguar appeared ill at ease. He constantly scanned the vegetation, turning completely around every fifteen or twenty paces, his brow furrowed, apparently sensing that something was amiss but unable to identify the cause.

The drug lord halted near the wall of foliage and turned his gaze to the sky, his hand idly playing in Maria's hair. She stood still, her arms still dangling, seemingly unconcerned by the treatment.

Bolan wished they had stayed where they were. He now had a longer shot to make, which didn't bother him quite as much as the fact Maria was farther away. When the crunch came, he'd be hard pressed to protect her. He noticed the radioman was talking into the receiver and nodding.

His walkie-talkie hissed to life.

"Mike, this is Keating. Do you copy?"

The warrior raised the device to his lips. "Yeah. Go ahead."

"I know I don't need to remind you not to make a move until I say the word. The chopper with our backup has just left the mainland and will be here in twenty minutes, but they won't close in until I see what's going down."

"Understood."

"Is that the woman you were telling us about?"

"Yes."

"I'll tell the others to avoid hitting her at all costs. Have you any idea why Espinosa brought her along?"

"None."

"Strange. Well, in any event we have the son of a bitch right where we want him. Wait for the word. Over and out."

Bolan deposited the radio on the ground and peered through the telescopic sight again. The game plan called for all the gunners to be taken out, if necessary, but for Espinosa to be spared to face trial. The DEA agents probably planned to milk their catch for all the rat was worth, parading Espinosa before the press and turning his trial into a three-ring circus. The publicity would do them a world of good, showing the public how efficient they were while at the same time enabling them to stress over and over again how badly they needed more funding and more men in the field. Typical.

The radioman unexpectedly produced a pair of binoculars from the backpack and handed them to Espinosa.

Flattening against the trunk, Bolan tensed, thinking Espinosa would train the binoculars on the vegetation. Instead he raised them skyward and swept the western horizon, verifying that a plane was coming in soon. A moment later the warrior saw it, a tiny black silhouette winging rapidly toward Trinity Island.

Party time.

12

The outline of the craft steadily expanded, acquiring the dimensions of a small, sleek airplane. It winged in low over the water, barely clearing the treetops, and banked sharply to the left, performing a tight loop that brought it around to the south side of the island. Without hesitation the pilot swooped toward the field.

Bolan had to admire the skill it took to bring the plane in, a feat only the most accomplished of flyers could perform. It passed almost directly overhead at the very moment the pilot killed the engine. The wheels touched down seconds after passing over the ring of woodland and settled down almost gently, the propeller still spinning, the wingtips bouncing slightly with the motion.

The plane rapidly crossed the field and stopped within ten feet of the reception committee. Not until the propeller ceased whirling did a door open and disgorge three heavily armed hardmen.

The additional gunners gave Bolan reason for concern, not for himself or the DEA agents but for Maria. The more hardmen there were, the greater the odds she would be hurt once the agents made their move. Counting Espinosa and the Jaguar, there were now ten men to take care of. Make that eleven.

Another man stepped from the plane, and it wasn't the pilot. A young, thin man with black, slicked-back hair, wearing slacks and a casual shirt shook hands with the Jaguar and then presented a brown briefcase to Espinosa, who accepted it as if he'd just received the Holy Grail. The newcomer gestured at Maria, and Espinosa made a remark that brought on wicked smiles all around.

In a way Bolan was disappointed. He'd hoped that the big man himself, Harmodio Remón, would show up, but from the looks of things a high-ranking subordinate had made the trip instead. There were several photographs of Remón in Brognola's file, and none matched the thin man. He saw the newcomer's men unload six more suitcases and stack them near Espinosa. There was no question as to what they contained.

The newcomer and Espinosa moved off to one side and engaged in a subdued discussion, their backs to their men.

Bolan glanced at the walkie-talkie, wondering what Keating was waiting for. There had to be over a hundred kilos of coke in those suitcases, enough evidence to put Espinosa away for years if the prosecution didn't bungle the case. He fixed the telescopic sight squarely on the Jaguar and waited for the word. A minute went by and nothing happened. He was about to call Keating and find out what was going on when Espinosa and the newcomer walked over to Maria.

The warrior placed his finger on the trigger and shifted the cross hairs from the man in black to Espinosa. The drug lord was speaking animatedly, and every now and then he pointed at Maria. The newcomer shook his head, at which point Espinosa shrugged and addressed one of the hardmen carrying an M-1.

Obediently the gunner seized Maria by the arm and drew her a few yards from the others, then stepped back and started to raise the M-1.

Bolan shifted the cross hairs a second time. He wasn't about to wait any longer. The angle was in his favor, and he was on the verge of squeezing off a shot when the DEA agents finally swung into action. Keating's voice barked the code word "Galahad," and Agent Seavers stood and bellowed a command.

"Drug Enforcement Agents. You're under arrest!"

All hell broke loose.

Some of the gunners snapped off hasty shots at Seavers. The guy with the M-1 whipped around in surprise, took in the situation at a glance, then turned to Maria and elevated the carbine.

The Executioner fired, and far across the field his target abruptly became jet propelled and hurtled through the air, narrowly missing Maria, only to prematurely crash to the ground within a yard of his takeoff.

Bolan shifted, the barrel braced against the tree for added support, smoothly worked the bolt to drive a fresh round into the chamber and drilled a second hardman in the head.

An all-out battle was in full swing. Every DEA agent had entered the fray, firing from concealment with lethal effect. The thin newcomer and one of his men were already down, but the rest were furiously returning fire while making for cover, dodging and weaving as they ran.

The warrior took a second look for Espinosa and the Jaguar, but neither man was in sight. He hadn't seen them take a hit, and there was no sign of them hiding in the weeds. Maria, incredibly, hadn't budged, and as his gaze lingered briefly on her face, he glimpsed someone rising directly behind her.

It was Espinosa, a pistol clenched in his right hand. He jammed the gun into Maria's temple and shouted, "Stop firing! Stop firing or the woman is history!"

All of the agents except Seavers complied.

"I'm warning you! I'll kill the bitch! Stop the damn firing now!"

The firebrand finally eased off the trigger.

For his part, Bolan was trying to get a clear shot at Espinosa, but the man was too smart to expose himself except for an eyebrow every few seconds as he twisted his head from side to side. The Executioner knew that one of the DEA agents was supposed to be in the trees somewhere to Espinosa's rear, and he hoped the agent would be able to get off a shot.

"Smart move!" the drug lord snapped, and glanced at the plane. The gunners had halted and were awaiting orders, but he ignored them and propelled Maria toward the aircraft.

Realizing Espinosa's intent, Bolan wished that someone had thought to take out the aircraft first. He wondered if one of the DEA agents might try anyway, and knew the first shot would result in Maria's death. But Keating must have spread the word that her life wasn't to be endangered, because Espinosa reached the plane and halted next to the open door, pivoting so his back was to the craft.

The Jaguar suddenly appeared, framed in the doorway, and assisted Espinosa in hauling the woman inside. In seconds the door slammed shut. Cries of alarm came from several of the gunners who belatedly awakened to the fact they were being abandoned. By then the pilot had the engine started and the aircraft roared into motion, swinging around and barreling down the field at top speed.

The cease-fire was suddenly off, and the agents cut loose with a vengeance, mowing down four hardmen in as many seconds.

Bolan had his eyes on the plane. He trained the Weatherby on the cockpit and had a perfect shot at the pilot, a shot he couldn't bring himself to take because of the consequences. A rare feeling welled up within him, a sense of helplessness mixed with a burning frustration at being thwarted when he'd almost rescued Maria.

Its engine whining, the plane rose into the cloudless sky and rapidly climbed to an altitude of one hundred feet before circling to the west.

The warrior whirled to discover the battle was already over. Only one gunner remained standing, and he was trying to touch the sun with his hands. Three of the agents were stepping from cover; Keating, Kuykendall and Seavers, but there was no sign of the fourth man, Williams.

Bolan moved across the field, joining the DEA agents as they converged quickly on the hardmen.

"Don't shoot!" the gunner yelled anxiously. "I give up! Don't shoot!"

Bodies lay scattered everywhere, most riddled by multiple impacts, a few groaning and twitching. Not one of the hardmen had escaped.

The agents reached the north end of the field a few seconds before Bolan. Since the operation was theirs, he stood by and covered them while they attended to checking each fallen gunner and Kuykendall slapped cuffs on the prisoner. His eyes flicked from body to body, and he saw one of the men who had arrived on the plane move an arm. The gunner was on his stomach, an M-16 lying within six inches of his right hand. But instead of reaching for the rifle, the man weakly groped at his waist for a grenade.

Bolan placed his foot on the gunner's wrist and held it there, pinning the man's arm. "Don't even think about it."

The hardman opened his eyes and glanced up, grimacing. Several exit wounds marked the back of his shirt above the waist. "Screw you, gringo!" he spit.

The warrior leaned down and relieved the man of his grenades and pistols. He wanted the guy to live a while longer, at least long enough to answer a few pertinent questions concerning Harmodio Remón's operation in Panama.

"What have we here?"

Bolan shifted to find Bill Keating approaching. "A live one," he replied. "Where's that chopper?"

"It'll be here any minute," Keating answered, studying the big man's face. "I'm sorry about the woman."

The warrior shrugged. "She got in over her head and paid the price."

"We tried our best to avoid harming her."

"I know."

Keating sighed and gazed to the west. "No one could have foreseen what happened."

Agent Seavers approached them at a dead run. "Bill, I found Willy in the trees. He took a round in the chest. He's still alive, but he won't make it unless we get him to a hospital pronto."

"I'll get on the horn and see what's keeping that helicopter. They can rush him to the mainland with the prisoners, and I'll have another bird fly in to pick up the dead," Keating said, turning. "Give Kuky a hand until I get back." He ran off toward the trees to the west.

Seavers glanced at the warrior. "Too bad about the woman, huh?"

Bolan remained silent.

"I mean, if not for her we would have bagged Espinosa. She cost us big, mister. I just hope she was worth it."

"Don't you have somewhere to go?"

The DEA agent's dark eyes narrowed. "Hey, what's with you, Belasko? I was only making conversation."

Bolan's next words were as hard as steel. "Make it somewhere else."

Seavers opened his mouth to voice a sarcastic retort, looked into the warrior's eyes and promptly decided to take the advice. He stalked off.

Mentally chiding himself for needlessly antagonizing the agent, Bolan glanced down at the hardman and frowned. Seavers had no idea that Bolan felt responsible for Maria. There was no reason for the Executioner to take out his anger on him.

As the gunner glared up at him, the Executioner toyed with the notion of interrogating the man on the spot. He needed critical information, and there lay the person who might be able to supply it. Only the realization that such questioning was better left to the professionals kept him in check.

Bolan stared westward and made up his mind about what had to be done. There was no getting around it. As soon as the prisoners were milked dry, he'd be on his way to Panama.

13

"So what did you find out?" Bolan asked as Hal Brognola entered his room at the Flamingo Motel.

The big man sank into a chair and regarded his friend intently. "We don't have everything yet, but there is some intel you'll like."

"I'm waiting." Bolan sat on the bed, in the act of cleaning his weapons.

"First I want to set the record straight. I don't like the idea of your going, but I won't stand in your way. If you think it's that important, I'll do whatever I can to help and provide support. Once you're in Panama, though, you'll be on your own."

"So what else is new?"

"You do realize you could be throwing your life away for nothing. Odds are that the woman is dead. Even if by some miracle you do find her alive, getting her out will be next to impossible. Remón has a small army of gunners on his payroll."

"The odds have never stopped us before," Bolan noted. "Besides, I'll have an edge. As far as they know, I'm dead. The element of surprise will be in my favor, and sometimes that's enough to even the odds."

"Sometimes."

Bolan looked at his friend. "I appreciate your concern, but I'm going. You've wanted to put Harmodio Remón out of operation for years. Here's your big chance."

"Yeah, but I'd prefer to initiate the operation, not have it forced on me."

The warrior decided to change the subject. "Fill me in on the interrogation."

"It went well. The guy who worked for Espinosa didn't know a whole hell of a lot, but the other one, a top gunner in Remón's organization, is a treasure trove of information. His name is Pedro Gallardo and he's been with Remón for seven years. He's supplied us with the address of Remón's hacienda located outside of Panama City, and pinpointed the general location of Remón's plantation in the province of Darien, where 220 acres are devoted to marijuana cultivation. The plantation is also a stepping-stone in the coke pipeline from the cartel to the U.S. Huge quantities are transported overland from Medellín to the plantation, and from there Remón's network distributes the drugs to points all around the globe."

"An operation as large as that would be impossible to cover up. The Panamanian authorities must know what's going on," Bolan commented.

"Yeah, they do, but the situation is the same there as it is in Colombia. The authorities have been either bought off, or they're unwilling to do anything for fear of what will happen to them or their families. Remón has politicians, judges, police officials, and even some prominent military officers in his back pocket. He greases their palms, and they conveniently look the other way or warn him if any honest investigator closes in," Brognola detailed.

"Sometimes it seems as if Central and South America are one big candy and pot store."

"You've got that right. A lot is made of the fact that Medellín is the heart of the cocaine trade, but hardly anyone ever brings up that Panama is one of the cartel's main money-laundering centers. At last count there were about one hundred and forty banks there holding upward of fifty billion in drug money. Hell, the cartel bigwigs travel to Panama City regularly and stay in the plushest hotels, right out in the open, and no one ever bothers them."

"What else did Gallardo tell you about Remón's empire?"

"That it's bigger than even we dreamed. If Gallardo is telling the truth, Remón is in a position to become *the* middleman in Central America."

"All the more reason for me to pay him a visit," Bolan said.

"We also learned a little about Remón himself. Like most of the big boys, and even with all the money he forks out under the table for protection, he's deathly afraid of being apprehended. He surrounds himself with a squad of highly trained gunners at all times, and I mean at *all* times. His bedroom at the hacienda and at the plantation are both surrounded by rooms housing gunners who work in shifts so there's always several awake and ready for action."

"Sounds like I have my work cut out for me," Bolan observed.

"There's more. We've also learned Remón is a real ladies' man. Keeps a stable of beauties on hand to service him nightly. Has a different woman every day. Gallardo claims that Remón likes to get them hooked on coke. He also said a few of the women disappeared without a trace, and he suspected Remón tired of them and had them killed."

The warrior thought of Maria and his features clouded.

"Apparently Remón never travels out of country. Not even to Colombia. Anyone who wants to do business with him has to go there, or else he sends a trusted lieutenant to arrange matters. If it's a major deal, he'll have the Jaguar handle the details. From what Gallardo says, the Jaguar is the only person Remón trusts completely."

Bolan's interest perked up. "Did the gunner say why?"

"He has no idea."

"There's more to that relationship than meets the eye."

"That'd be my guess. Anyway, we also learned Remón is a big fan of the cockfights. Attends one every Friday night and does some heavy gambling, but doesn't seem to mind if he loses. He just likes to see the gamecocks tear each other apart."

"Interesting. I can use that."

"Figured you would."

"Sounds to me as if Gallardo spilled his guts. How did you persuade him to talk?"

"Oh, I applied a little leverage," Brognola said evasively.

"What kind of leverage?"

The big Fed gazed out the window. "Amnesty."

Glancing up in surprise, Bolan lowered the Weatherby to the bed and placed the cleaning cloth and rod next to it. "You did what?"

"I offered him unconditional amnesty from prosecution if he would come clean."

"That's not like you."

Brognola shrugged. "It was either that or nothing. The only way he would cooperate was if we agreed to let him go afterward and feed the word back through the grapevine that he'd died from his wounds, just in case Remón should think of looking for him."

"You were a little generous, if you ask me."

"You wanted the intel, didn't you?"

"Yes," Bolan said, and suddenly understood. Brognola had made such a sweeping deal for his sake, knowing how much he needed the information if he was to have any hope of finding Maria Salvato. The big Fed would rather have sent Gallardo to the slammer for ten or twenty years, not pardoned him. "I owe you one," the Executioner stated.

"You owe me diddly."

Bolan smiled and slid off the bed. "How soon can I leave?"

"Tomorrow morning. You're already booked under the name of Mike Belasko. When you arrive in

Panama City, a contact will be waiting to meet you. His name is Rodrigo Bonilla, a former officer with the Panamanian Defense Forces. He's clean, and he's helped us out on several occasions.''

"Okay."

"There's more. As you know, the DEA has agents in Panama. One of them reported to Bill Keating that Antonio Espinosa is in Panama City, apparently as a houseguest of Remón's. It's too bad the coast guard couldn't catch them before they flew out of American jurisdiction.''

"Did this agent mention a woman answering Maria's description?"

"No."

"I noticed her name wasn't mentioned in the papers.''

"The DEA press release on the bust describes her as an unidentified woman for good reason. Do you know what the media would do with a story about a mother who turned vigilante to avenge the drug death of her son and then was abducted, possibly to Panama? The networks, the talk shows and the papers would milk it for all it was worth. We'd have demagogues in Congress calling for military intervention. The administration would be on the hot seat. Do we really want that to happen?''

Bolan said nothing.

"As far as the public is concerned, Maria Salvato is missing and presumed killed in the explosion that tore apart her brownstone and severely damaged two others.''

"In other words, she's left high and dry."

"Not exactly," Brognola said, and grinned. "She has you."

A shadow seemed to flit across the big man's face. "I just hope I'm enough."

WHEN MACK BOLAN—alias Mike Belasko—entered the crowded terminal at Tocumen Airport outside Panama City, he presented the image of a typical American tourist. A sport shirt and slacks clothed his muscular six-foot-three-inch frame, and a camera dangled from around his neck. He reclaimed his luggage, a single suitcase, and went through customs. As he slid his fake passport into his pants pocket, a nearby loudspeaker blared to life.

"Will Mr. Mike Belasko please report to the information counter by the main entrance?"

The warrior threaded a path through the lobby until he spied the counter in question, and right away he made his contact, a stocky man with white hair and a bristling mustache who was standing off to one side and scanning the crowd. He walked over to the attractive brunette behind the counter. "Hello. My name is Belasko. I believe you paged me."

"Yes, I did," the woman responded politely, and looked at the stocky man. "Señor Bonilla, here is the gentleman you wanted."

Bonilla stepped over and warmly shook Bolan's hand. "Mr. Belasko. I trust your flight was pleasant?"

"Very."

"I have a car," Bonilla said, gesturing at the glass doors. "If you would follow me."

They walked from the terminal and turned to the south, sticking to the sidewalk as they headed for a parking lot.

Bonilla glanced up at the big American. "I haven't been told why you are here, and I don't want to know. Understand?"

"Yes," Bolan replied.

The Panamanian scanned their immediate vicinity to make certain no one could overhear them. "I did my best to fill the shopping list our mutual friend gave me, but Panama isn't the U.S. Such items are harder to come by. I trust you will be satisfied with the selection."

"Were you able to get the fruit?"

"Yes, half a dozen of the finest grade pineapples. I threw in a few extra items for good measure," Bonilla added. He led the way to a nondescript gray Ford and unlocked the driver's door.

Bolan stood next to the passenger side and gazed at the sky, the city and the terminal, pretending to be taking in the sights while he checked to see if they were being tailed. There were plenty of people moving to and from the entrance, but no one who set off warning bells in his mind. He heard the click of his door being unlocked and climbed in, twisting so he could toss the suitcase into the back seat.

"You have a room booked at the Hotel El Grande," Bonilla mentioned as he started the car. "I envy you.

It is one of the best in the world. The ladies who frequent the pool can make a grown man drool."

The warrior grinned. "Are you an avid swimmer?"

"No, *señor.* My wife would kill me if I so much as dip my little toe in the water. Are you married?"

Bolan shook his head.

"How convenient. For the right price you can take your pick of swimming companions." Bonilla backed from the parking space and headed for the exit. "Although, if your shopping list is any indication, you won't have much time for water sports."

The warrior surveyed the parking area and saw a green Mercedes pull from a slot and follow them at a respectable distance. There were two men in the front seat, both wearing dark suits and sunglasses. "Where are the items you obtained for me?" he asked.

"In the trunk."

"Do you have any hardware up front?"

Bonilla nodded at the glove compartment. "There's a pistol in there. Why?"

"Because we might need it."

14

Fifteen minutes later Bonilla made a turn onto the avenue bordering the Hotel El Grande and glanced in the rearview mirror. "They are still behind us. Do you want me to try to lose them?"

"No. They're my problem. Just let me off in front of the hotel."

"What about the car and your gear?"

"The car isn't yours?"

"No, *señor.* I was instructed to find a vehicle for your personal use, one the police won't be able to trace should there be any unfortunate accidents."

Bolan pondered for a minute. "Then give me a call in thirty minutes and let me know where I can pick it up. Leave the keys under the carburetor cover."

"Are you sure? I am willing to help you dispose of them."

The warrior detected the longing of an old soldier who missed all the action. "I'm sure," he stressed. "Our mutual friend might have need of your services again, and he'd be pretty upset if I let you get involved."

"As you wish."

The Hotel El Grande turned out to be a magnificent, ultramodern, fifteen-story tribute to Latin American architecture. Every room above ground level sported a white balcony. Those on the south side overlooked the Olympic-size swimming pool in which frolicked a bevy of beauties, men of all ages and the inevitable contingent of noisy tourists.

Bolan surveyed the pool as his contact brought the car to a stop at the curb. He retrieved his suitcase, placed it in his lap and tapped the glove compartment. "Mind if I take the pistol?"

"Everything in this car is yours to do with as you please."

A flick of a circular knob opened the glove compartment to reveal a Taurus Model PT 92, a compact 9 mm pistol with a four-inch barrel. Small, but it packed a solid punch. Bolan palmed the weapon, verified the clip was full and placed the gun in his suitcase.

"I trust it is satisfactory?" Bonilla asked.

"It will do nicely."

Bolan slid out and paused before slamming the door. "Thirty minutes, amigo."

"*Si, señor.* And good luck. You will need it."

The warrior went into the hotel without glancing at the Mercedes. He knew it had pulled to the curb a block away, and he didn't want them to know that he was aware of the tail. They'd find out soon enough. Crossing the spacious, ornate lobby, he halted at the front desk. "Mike Belasko. I believe you have a reservation in my name."

"One moment, sir. I'll check."

Bolan idly scanned the lobby but saw no one who aroused suspicion. Good. If the opposition didn't have someone planted in the hotel, it would make his job a lot easier.

"Here we go, Mr. Belasko," the clerk declared, returning with a key in her left hand and a registration form in her right. "You have room 117, and you're very lucky it's available."

"I am?"

"Oh, yes sir. Ground-floor rooms are usually booked solid at this time of year. I noticed on the reservation slip that you specifically requested one."

Bolan reasoned that Brognola must have arranged for a ground-floor room so he could slip in and out of the window, if need be, to avoid attracting attention. He filled out the registration form and and took the key. A bellboy materialized at his elbow. He let the suitcase be taken and followed the bellboy to room 117, which was located on the north side of the hotel.

After dispensing a tip and locking the door, Bolan conducted a manual check for bugs. After conducting his sweep, he peered out the window to find a narrow strip of grass and shrubbery, and beyond that the hotel parking lot. Perfect.

Bolan sat in a chair near the phone and waited for the call from Bonilla. He spent the time pondering the latest development and plotting his strategy. As someone who had spent all of his adult life as a professional soldier, either in or out of uniform, he preferred the direct approach when dealing with enemies.

Clandestine activities like elaborate covers, playing follow the leader with tails, and all the rest of the secret-agent routines were not his forte. But this time he didn't have much choice. He couldn't just barge into Remón's hacienda in the hope Maria was there. Necessity dictated he take it slow and outthink the opposition.

Which brought him around to the guys in the Mercedes. How had they latched on to him so quickly? Or had they been shadowing Bonilla all along? Were they Remón's men or working for someone else? Whoever they were, he'd let them play their game for the time being. If he took them out now, before he was ready to make his move, he'd alert whoever sent them.

Tomorrow was Friday, and that evening Remón would attend the cockfights. There would be fewer gunners at the hacienda since Remón always took a troop of bodyguards wherever he went. It would be the ideal time to search the place for Maria.

Bolan tried not to think about whether she was still alive. He simply took it for granted that she was. Knowing the type of men Remón and Espinosa were, he could well imagine the ordeal she'd been through. Even if she survived, she'd be emotionally scarred for life.

The warrior glanced at his watch, noted there were fifteen minutes until the call was due, and rose. He opened the suitcase and removed the Taurus and two maps, one of Panama, the other a large-scale depiction of Panama City, both courtesy of Brognola. He pinpointed the hacienda's address on the west side of the city and mentally reviewed the route he would take. Engrossed in memorizing the details, he was pleasantly surprised when the phone rang five minutes ahead of schedule. In two strides he scooped the receiver to his ear. "Hello."

"Señor Belasko, this is Bonilla."

"Any problems?"

"No, *señor.* Our escort didn't follow me, and none of their friends showed up."

"Good. What about the transportation?"

"There is a store at the corner of Balboa Boulevard and Roble Street."

"Understood."

"Take care, *señor.*"

Bolan hung up and moved to the map. He found the intersection Bonilla had mentioned, then settled down to wait until dark. In his line of work, night was a man's best friend.

THE NIGHTLIFE of Panama was in full swing when Bolan hit the streets. He stopped every now and then to make certain he wasn't being followed. He carried the city map in a back pocket, and finding the intersection of Balboa and Roble proved to be easy. The car was parked at the northeast corner of the lot, well away from the store. The warrior waited until there was no one in the immediate vicinity, then popped the hood and retrieved the keys. He went into the store and purchased a loaf of bread, meat and cheese, and carried the shopping bag to the trunk. If anyone should be watching, they'd see a gringo storing his groceries, nothing more.

The warrior unlocked the trunk and raised the lid. Spread out on a blue blanket were the weapons Bonilla had obtained. There were the six fragmentation grenades, four smokers, enough 9 mm ammo to start a war, a Madsen M-46 and a SIG 510-4 rifle. The Madsen was a 9 mm submachine gun widely used by security forces in Central and South America; they were quite common in Brazil, Paraguay, Colombia, Guatemala and El Salvador. Bolan had used Madsens before and rated them as top-notch.

The rifle was a welcome bonus to the little arsenal. Although the SIG 510-4's muzzle velocity and rate of fire were a third less than an M-16's, it was a lethal piece of firepower in the traditional NATO caliber of 7.62 mm. No tools were required for fieldstripping, and the rifle came complete with a bipod that could be folded up against the barrel casing. The armed forces of Chile and Bolivia both used them.

Bolan deposited the shopping bag next to a stack of spare magazines for the rifle and closed the trunk. In moments he was on his way to the hotel, adhering strictly to the traffic laws to avoid being pulled over. When he went past the front of the brightly illuminated El Grande, the Mercedes was nowhere in sight. He wondered if the shadows had called it a night or gone to feed their faces. There were few vehicles in the north lot when he braked in a space directly out from his window.

Bolan climbed out, locked the door and opened the trunk. He placed a box of 9 mm ammo in the shopping bag, secured the lid and strolled casually to the hotel entrance. A new desk clerk was on duty, and she gave Bolan only a perfunctory glance and nod as he went by.

He reached 117 and drew the room key from his pocket. He glanced both ways, saw only innocent tourists farther down the hall and unlocked the door. Taking a stride inside, he reached for the light switch, but before his fingers could touch it the door swung shut. A pair of strong arms seized him around the legs at the same instant a garrote slipped around his neck.

15

The Executioner instinctively inhaled deeply and exploded into action, throwing himself to the right and taking both hardmen with him, not giving the killers a chance to brace themselves. His knees were clamped together by the guy down low so he couldn't stop himself from falling. As he fell, with the garrote gouging into his throat, he released the shopping bag and swept both arms up and around, his hands closing on a pair of sturdy wrists. Using his own momentum as leverage, he bent at the waist and heaved.

Killer number one sailed up and over, trying desperately to retain his grip on the garrote but losing his hold when his body slammed into the wall with enough force to crack the plaster.

Bolan landed on his right side and twisted, lancing both rigid hands at the vague outline of a head near his knees. He smacked his palms against the man's ears, and suddenly his legs were free as killer number two let go and tumbled backward.

Temporarily in the clear, Bolan jumped to his feet and tore the garrote from his neck. He seized the ends and spun to meet the charge of the first assailant, who came at him swinging a vicious right, the fist barely visible in the gloom. Deftly sidestepping, Bolan looped the garrote around the hardman's neck in a smooth, practiced motion, then stepped in behind the killer, which put them back to back, and whipped his body at the floor while hauling on the cord.

Again killer number one flew over the warrior's shoulder, only this time feet first, to crash onto the floor with a distinct crack from his leg left.

Bolan's arm's bulged as he yanked on the garrote. He felt a fist strike him ineffectually in the stomach, and then the hardman was clawing at his hands. Gritting his teeth, the warrior tried to bury the cord in the killer's neck, knowing he had to hurry, that the second hardman could take him out at any second.

Killer number two pounced from behind, wrapping an arm around the Executioner's windpipe.

Automatically Bolan brought both arms up, saving his life with the movement as he inadvertently blocked the killer's knife hand. He grabbed the wrist and shoved, propelling them both half a dozen feet to stumble into a chair.

They both went down, the warrior on top.

Bolan drove his left elbow back once, twice, three times, and with the final blow the pressure on his neck slackened and he was able to jerk free. With both feet on the floor, he rotated, jamming the assailant's knife arm against his leg, then clamped his other hand on the guy's wrist and tried to snap it.

Killer number two lashed out with his foot.

The tip of the shoe caught Bolan in the ribs, eliciting a grunt. He saw the hardman trying to sit up, and he flicked his own leg out, the heel catching the killer in the face and rocking him. A second snap kick crunched teeth and his adversary abruptly went limp.

Bolan slid the knife from the man's slack fingers and straightened. He drew the Taurus and turned to the light, warily watching both prostrate figures, but checked his intent when a tentative knock sounded on the door.

Someone spoke a few muffled words in inquiry in Spanish.

"Coming," Bolan responded, and standing so his body would block a view of the interior he opened the door a few inches, careful to keep the pistol and knife out of sight. "Yes?"

A middle-aged man and woman, both Panamanians, eyed him quizzically. "Pardon me," the man said. "My wife and I were going by your room when we heard some loud noises. Are you all right?"

"Fine, thank you."

The woman craned her neck in an effort to see inside. "Are you sure? We can notify the manager if you're having any problems."

"I'm fine," Bolan reiterated. He suspected the woman might inform the manager anyway and decided to nip her curiosity in the bud. "To tell you the truth," he said, adopting a sheepish expression, "I dozed off earlier and just woke up. On my way to the bathroom I tripped over a chair and nearly broke my leg." He paused for effect. "I feel like an idiot."

The husband nodded knowingly. "I know what you mean. I've lost count of the number of times I've stubbed my toe or banged my leg in the dark."

"Thanks for inquiring, though," Bolan added. "Your kindness is appreciated. Most folks nowadays don't want to get involved with strangers."

"Well, sorry to bother you," the husband stated, and started off.

"No problem," Bolan said, smiling at the wife, and was relieved when she grinned and departed. Closing and locking the door, he finally switched on the overhead light and studied the hardmen.

Killer number one was history, his tongue protruding from his mouth, his wide eyes fixed on the ceiling.

His companion had a broken nose, a split lip, and other facial injuries, but he was alive and breathing heavily.

Bolan walked into the bathroom and filled a glass with tap water, then returned to his uninvited guest. Upending it, he trained the pistol on the hardman as the water splashed on the guy's eyes and into his open mouth.

Spitting blood and coughing, the hardman awakened abruptly and sat up, covering his mouth with his hands. He blinked, remembered where he was and looked up in horror at Bolan's grim visage.

The warrior backed off a yard to give himself room to maneuver in case the hardman got any fancy ideas.

The killer started to rise.

"Stay where you are," Bolan barked.

About to voice a reply, the man's eyes strayed to his companion and he went rigid, swallowing hard.

"Do you want to wind up like your buddy?" Bolan inquired.

"No."

"Then cooperate and you might get to live."

"What do you want?"

"Information. First, what's your name?"

"Alfredo Gallegos."

"Do you work for Harmodio Remón?"

Gallegos glanced up, but hesitated, evidently thinking of the consequences if he betrayed his boss.

"You have two choices," Bolan said harshly. "You can tell me what I want to know and live, or don't and die." He extended the pistol. "Do you work for Remón?"

"Yes, I do."

"He sent you to kill me?"

"No. The Jaguar did. Do you know who he is?"

"We've met," Bolan said.

"And you're still alive?"

"I'll ask the questions. How did the Jaguar know I was coming to Panama?"

"I don't think he did."

"Don't lie to me," the warrior snapped. "Your buddy and you were on my tail the moment I landed."

Nervously licking his bleeding lip, the gunner nodded. "True, but we followed you because your name is one of those on the list and we heard you being paged."

"List?"

"Yes. You see, Mr. Remón is not the kind of man who takes chances. He keeps two men out at the airport at all times. Several of the employees there are on the payroll, and they supply passenger manifests to us. We compare the names on the manifests to the list the Jaguar gives us of certain persons who might be entering or leaving the country."

"How many names are on this list?"

"It varies from time to time. About twenty-five at the moment. Your name was just added a day or two ago."

"And how did the Jaguar learn my name?"

The killer's shoulders bounced. "I can only guess that he got it from the woman."

Bolan was next to the man in a flash, the pistol almost touching what was left of the guy's nose. "What woman?"

"An American with dark hair. I don't know her name."

"Where is she now?"

"At Remón's hacienda. She is locked in one of the rooms in the basement."

"And she's still alive?"

"The last I knew."

The warrior backed up. For some reason Remón was keeping Maria alive. But for how long? If he waited until tomorrow night to go in, it might be too late. He glanced at the clock on the night table.

With surprising speed, the hardman came off the floor and leaped, his arms extended, his fingers hooked into claws.

Bolan simply twisted, jammed the Taurus into the hardman's ribs and squeezed the trigger. The booming retort was muffled by the guy's body, and he was dead before he hit the carpet.

Now what? Bolan sat on the bed and thoughtfully regarded the corpses. Once the men failed to report in, the Jaguar was bound to send out another hit team. And since his cover was blown all to hell, there was no reason to pussyfoot around any longer. Waiting another day until the cockfights was pointless. Time for the direct approach.

The Executioner knew he'd have to move quickly. If he could get to the hacienda in an hour or so, he might catch them napping. In any event, getting Maria out would have to be done the old-fashioned hard way. Which suited him just fine.

All he had to do now was to get rid of the bodies.

CLAD IN BLACK SLACKS and a black sweatshirt, his arsenal on the seat beside him, Bolan drove down Veraguas Avenue at the speed limit so as not to arouse suspicion, passing Harmodio Remón's estate on the right. He didn't like what he saw.

A chain-link fence surrounded the four-acre plot on which the palatial house sat. There were guards at the front gate, and floodlights positioned at regular intervals all around the property. Those lights revealed a lot of activity. Two military-type convoy trucks were parked near the house, and a dozen men were busily engaged in loading boxes and crates on board. Overseeing the operation was a familiar figure in a black suit—the Jaguar.

Bolan went to the next intersection and took a right. Few homes were in the area, affording Remón a degree of privacy. The big man suspected that the homeowners who did live nearby had been bought off or else they were too scared to contact the police when they noticed unusual activities on the drug lord's property. He drove twenty yards and pulled over beside a strand of trees that effectively screened the Ford from the hacienda.

Next the warrior loaded up. Bonilla had provided standard-issue military webbing, and Bolan clipped on the smoke grenades and four of the fragmentation grenades. As much ammo as he could carry was crammed into pouches. The Madsen was slung over his left shoulder, and he cradled the SIG 510-4 as he slid out. The Taurus once again nestled at the small of his back.

Bolan scanned the stretch of woodland across the road, then gazed to the east at the lights of a home half a mile away. Except for the fading taillights of a vehicle to the south, there was no traffic. He hunched over and moved to the stand, taking cover behind a tree trunk in order to study the layout of the grounds.

Beyond the stand was a flat strip no more than five yards wide, then the chain-link fence. To the right, perhaps thirty feet, reared one of the floods on a high pole. To the left, half that distance, was another. The grass, trees and shrubbery were brightly illuminated.

There appeared to be no way to gain entry without being spotted. Bolan frowned and scanned the length of the fence, seeking a point of weakness. He guessed that Remón owned much more land than the four acres, but only the house rated the added protection. Not that a chain-link fence was much of a deterrent. A brick or stone wall would have been better. He wondered if the fence was electrified. At the very least, there had to be hidden alarms at strategic intervals.

Bolan crawled to the edge of the stand, looked to the left and froze.

A hardman was patrolling the perimeter, an M-16 in the crook of one arm, and he gave the impression of being bored.

The warrior eased behind a bush, his mind racing. There were no other gunners in sight, and there was enough cover between the fence and the house to conceal him if he could get on that side. A big *if*. But short of a frontal assault, he had to adapt to the circumstances and this was his best bet.

The guard came closer, yawning and gazing at the stars.

Bolan waited until the man was abreast of his position, then made his move.

16

In the act of yawning again, the sentry froze with his mouth wide when a big man in black burst from cover and trained a rifle on his midriff. He looked into the chilling eyes of the stranger and saw instant death if he so much as flinched.

"Put the hardware on the ground. Slowly."

The sentry complied, then straightened and started to elevate his arms.

"Did I tell you to do that?" the big man growled. "Put your hands down."

Nodding vigorously, the sentry obeyed. He realized the stranger stood directly in front of him so that anyone gazing in their direction from the house might not notice there were two men instead of one.

"Touch the fence."

"Pardon?"

"Touch the fence and be quick about it."

Dutifully the guard stepped closer and placed his right hand on the chain links. Only then did he comprehend the intruder was checking to see if the fence was electrified.

"Now move back two paces."

He retreated the required distance.

Bolan craned his neck to scrutinize the hacienda and the grounds. After a few seconds he nodded at the grass. "Okay. When I say the word, you're to turn around and face the house until I tell you otherwise. Understand?"

"Yes."

"Keep your arms at your sides and look relaxed."

"Please don't kill me."

"What I do depends on you."

"I will do whatever you want."

The big man glanced at the house again. "Now!" he commanded.

Instantly the guard wheeled.

The fence suddenly rattled and shook.

Tensing, the gunner guessed that the big man had jumped up, caught hold of the top bar, and was entering the grounds. For a few moments the man would be vulnerable. He was tempted to make a grab for the M-16, but before he could work up the courage a hard object gouged him in the back and the steely voice spoke again.

"Start walking."

Amazed at how fast the stranger moved, the guard headed toward the house. He went past a few trees, several rose bushes and went to skirt a cluster of bamboo.

"Have a nice nap."

The guard experienced a fleeting, intense pain on the side of his head and everything faded to black.

BOLAN ADVANCED SLOWLY, his senses primed, taking advantage of the shrubbery to conceal his approach. So far he hadn't detected any magic-eye alarms, but that didn't mean they weren't there. Remón had to have the grounds wired. Such an oversight in so cautious a man would be inexplicable. Unless, of course, Remón relied more on manpower than technology. Unlike Antonio Espinosa, who seemed to like high-tech gadgetry, Remón might belong to the old school that believed the solution to every problem and security situation was sheer firepower.

On the east side of the house the hardmen were still loading the trucks. Conversations in Spanish wafted on the breeze.

The warrior came to a waist-high hedge and flattened. He crouch-walked to the west end and peeked out at the backyard, relieved there wasn't a gunner in sight. The loading operation worked in his favor, involving hardmen who otherwise might be patrolling the property.

Bolan scanned the windows and saw several illuminated from within, but they were each covered with draperies. There were two doors, one at the nearest corner, another midway along the wall. He stood erect and sprinted to the house, expecting to hear an alarm or a shout, and reached the closest door without incident. A tentative twist of the knob revealed it was unlocked, and with a last glance at the grounds he slipped into a darkened hallway and shut the door.

So far, so good.

Stealthily advancing toward a door rimmed by cracks of light, the warrior felt a puff of cool air on his left cheek and turned. Another, open door led down to the basement, the steps and the walls difficult to perceive in the gloom. He went to the third step, then closed the door.

From somewhere below came a low groan.

Bolan descended quickly, his back to the wall. At the bottom he groped along the wall until his fingers touched a light switch. He hesitated, aware of the risk he took, then flicked it on.

A huge basement was illuminated, filled with boxes piled in stacks on the left side and rows of workbenches and tables on the right. Those he ignored, surprised to discover three large cages occupying the space in the middle. Two of the cages contained prisoners, both women, and one was Maria Salvato.

Bolan stepped to the steel bars and crouched. "Maria?" he whispered.

It was doubtful she even knew he was there. She sat propped against the rear bars, her eyes open but unfocused, her features slack, still wearing the same clothes she'd had on when last Bolan saw her, only now they were rumpled and grimy. Her arms dangled listlessly, her fingers twitching every now and then.

"Maria?" Bolan repeated urgently.

The other woman, a pretty dark-haired Panamanian wearing a torn yellow dress, stirred and looked up, blinking rapidly. "Who are you?" she croaked.

"A friend," Bolan whispered. "I'm here to get you out."

The woman laughed weakly. "You're crazy. There is no escape from Harmodio."

"Where are the keys to the cages?"

"Over there," the woman said, feebly pointing at the wall.

Pivoting, the warrior spied a key ring hanging from a nail. He retrieved it and returned to Maria's cage, inspecting each of half a dozen keys to determine which would fit the lock.

"I must be dreaming," the Panamanian said.

"I'm for real," Bolan assured her.

The warrior inserted a key, then another, and on the second try the cage door swung outward. He knelt beside Maria, slipped an arm around her shoulders and shook her gently. "Maria, it's Mike. You've got to snap out of it. Can you hear me?"

Her only reaction was to blink once.

"You're wasting your time," the other woman advised. "They fried her brain with drugs."

Bolan scowled. Every second he wasted increased the chance of being detected. He went to the Panamanian's cage and unlocked the door. "Can you walk?"

"Yes."

"Give me a hand with Maria and we'll all escape in one piece."

"My name is Theodora," the woman disclosed as she slowly stepped out. Pausing, she gripped the bars for support. "They have not fed me in over a day and a half."

"What did you do to deserve such treatment?" Bolan inquired, walking back to Maria.

"Harmodio wanted me to be one of his women. At first I was flattered, but the more I thought about it, the more I saw what kind of man he truly was, the less I liked the idea. So I told him I was leaving." Her voice lowered. "He resented my attitude."

The warrior slung the rifle over his right shoulder and lifted Maria. She moved her lips but no sounds came out. He recalled how vibrant she'd been in Miami, the fleeting feel of her kiss, and grit his teeth in anger. "I'll carry her to the top of the stairs," he told Theodora.

"I can manage from there."

Bolan went up quickly. He set Maria on her feet and propped her against the wall, then unslung the Madsen and cracked the door. The empty hall offered encouragement. If the hardmen would only keep busy loading the trucks, he could pull it off. He glanced at Theordora, placed a finger over his lips to caution her to silence and eased through the doorway.

Despite her professed doubts about their prospects, Theodora was equal to the job at hand. She looped both arms around Maria, grunted and hauled her along. Maria shuffled awkwardly, as if deep down she sensed what they were trying to do and wanted to help.

The warrior moved to the outer door and checked the lawn. There were no guards, no alarms. He beckoned for Theodora to hurry, then covered them as they stepped outside. A beeline for the car was their best bet. Holding the Madsen in his right hand, he circled

Maria's waist with his left and assisted in propelling
her toward the hedge.

Bolan scanned right and left, front and back,
knowing this was the moment when they were most
vulnerable. He mentally ticked off the yards to the
shrubbery, and they still had five to go when a sharp
cry to their left caused all hell to break loose. He let go
of Maria and spun, leveling the Madsen, thinking a
guard had spotted them. Instead a shadowy silhouette at a second-floor window shouted again.

The warrior stitched a short burst across the pane.
Glass shattered, and the silhouette shrieked and toppled backward. He grabbed Maria again, almost
tearing her from Theodora's grasp as they sped to the
hedge and paused. "Get to the fence."

"What about you?"

"I'll buy you the time you need."

Theodora didn't debate the point. She hastened off,
straining to brace Maria, and disappeared behind
some shrubs.

Shouts arose in front of the hacienda.

Bolan turned toward the house and saw a pair of
gunners racing around the southeast corner. He
squatted next to the hedge, gripped a fragmentation
grenade and let them get a little closer. If he could
draw all the attention to himself, the women might
make the fence unmolested. Placing the submachine
gun at his feet, he cupped the grenade in his right
hand, his thumb holding the safety lever down and
pulled the pin. In a fluid motion he rose above the

hedge and hurled the grenade, falling prone the instant it left his fingers.

The blast and concussion blew out every window on that side of the house.

Rising before the dust settled, Bolan tucked the Madsen against his ribs and backpedaled.

Another gunner popped out at the far end of the building.

The warrior elevated the barrel to compensate for the distance and sent slugs ripping through the hardman's chest, then darted to a rosebush and crouched. He unclipped two of the smoke grenades, and when more gunners pounded into view at both corners he tossed the smokers at the hedge.

Dense white smoke poured from the canisters, creating a screening cloud in seconds.

Bolan whirled and sprinted after the women. The smoke grenades would spew their HC mixture for about two and a half minutes and hopefully delay Remón's crew.

Directly ahead a scream pierced the sounds of battle.

Dreading the worst, Bolan raced past the bamboo and spotted Maria and Theodora ten feet from the fence, two gunners on their right. A tall hardman glanced in his direction, and Bolan launched into a dive, jarring his elbows on the ground as hot lead sailed overhead.

The warrior took down the tall gunner first, aiming carefully so as not to hit the women, and rolled before the guy's comrade could nail his hide.

Theodora protectively placed both arms around Maria and bent down.

Surging up, Bolan bored the second gunner between the shoulder blades as the guy raced for cover, then the warrior jogged to the fence.

"How am I going to get her over?" Theodora wailed. "She's too heavy."

"Let me," Bolan said, shouldering the Madsen. He draped Maria over his right shoulder and began to climb, the metal links gouging into his hands, the strain in his shoulders tremendous. By pressing his soles flat on the fence and pulling, he succeeded in reaching the upper bar. Now came the hard part. Shifting his shoulder, he slid Maria onto the fence, her body bent at the waist, her legs on the inside, her arms out. It had to hurt her stomach but couldn't be helped. Swinging his right leg over, he sat up, balanced on the bar and gestured at the Panamanian. "Grab my hand."

As she raised her arms, Bolan glanced at the grounds.

A lone guard charged toward them, elevated an Armalite AR-18 and fired.

17

Theodora gasped and arched her spine as the rounds perforated her back and hurled her into the fence.

At the very millisecond the guard cut loose, Bolan grabbed for the Taurus. The gunner made a mistake in nailing the woman first instead of him, and he capitalized on the error. Just as the Armalite barrel started to track upward, the Executioner cored the guard's brain with a single shot. Looking down, he saw Theodora slumped against the links.

The warrior scanned the grounds, then got his arms under Maria and lowered her to the grass. He alighted beside her, tucked the pistol under his belt and carried her through the trees to the car, where he placed her gently on the back seat. Once behind the wheel, he gunned the engine and floored the accelerator.

Finally he could relax a bit. Repeated checks in the rearview mirror showed no pursuit. Trees lined the desolate stretch of road ahead, and he pushed the speedometer up to seventy, rapidly leaving Remón's estate far behind.

His next step would be to contact Brognola and arrange to have Maria taken out of the country. Since she'd entered illegally and lacked the proper papers, the Justice man's operatives would be useful in spiriting her to the U.S. with a minimum of legal hassles. He toyed with the notion of persuading Brognola to supply her with a new identity once she recovered. After the hell she'd been through, she deserved to be able to start her life over, free of Espinosa's or Remón's retribution.

Bolan absently glanced in the mirror again, his hands tightening on the steering wheel when he spied a pair of headlights. Bringing the speedometer up to eighty, he looked again, hoping it was just one of the locals heading home from the city.

The headlights closed swiftly, as if they were attached to a rocket instead of a car.

No local would drive that fast, Bolan reflected. Remón or the Jaguar must have sent cars out in all directions, but what kind of cars? The pursuit vehicle appeared to be doing more than one hundred. In less than a minute it would overtake him.

An intersection came into view.

Bolan spun the wheel, taking the car to the right, and found himself on a gravel road. Clouds of dust swirled from under the tires as he stamped on the gas pedal. The dust would reveal which branch he took, but it would also reduce the pursuing driver's visibility and perhaps force the man to slow down.

The warrior rolled down his window, letting the cool air stroke his brow, and scanned the terrain on both sides for a spot to pull over. Rather than try to outrun the chase car, he'd put the pursuers out of action. A break in the heavy underbrush on the left side offered an ideal spot. He buried the brake pedal and executed a sharp turn, the tail end slewing briefly before he left the road and pulled into a narrow clearing. Stopping, he shut off the engine and took the time to slap a full magazine into the Madsen, then slid out of the vehicle.

Bolan listened to the roar of the pursuit car, which tapered to a metallic growl when the driver made the turn, then sprinted to the edge of the undergrowth and sank to one knee. Suspended dust particles still hung like a shroud above the road. Refracted circles of light appeared, zooming nearer. He sighted the SIG 510-4 on a point above the headlights and waited.

When they were within a guaranteed kill zone, he squeezed off deliberately spaced shots, going for the windshield, contriving to take out the driver and cause the uncontrolled vehicle to crash. Six shots blasted from the rifle before realization dawned.

Not one of the rounds penetrated the glass.

Bulletproofed. Bolan fired with the same result at the side windows as the brown car sped past him.

With the brakes squealing in protest, the driver brought the vehicle to an abrupt halt, slanting the front end across the road.

The warrior reached for a grenade. Out of the corner of his eye he glimpsed another pair of headlights approaching from the intersection. Somewhere along the line a second car had joined the chase, or maybe it had been there all along following so closely behind the first vehicle that its lights hadn't been visible.

Whatever the case, he was caught between the proverbial rock and hard place. If he stayed where he was, stray bullets might hit the Ford. He had to lead them away from Maria.

Surging from cover, Bolan sprinted across the road, letting his enemies see him, palming a grenade as he reached the other side. Already gunners were spilling from the first car. He yanked on the pin, heaved the bomb and dived into the weeds.

Panicked shouts broke out, attended by a flurry of stamping feet, all capped by the explosion.

Bolan hugged the ground as a fireball mushroomed skyward accompanied by the grating discord of tortured metal. He rose to a crouch and angled toward a tree.

The second car screeched to a stop and hardmen poured out, fanning right and left.

Hopeless odds called for desperate measures, and Bolan took a bold gamble. From behind the tree he snapped off a few shots to temporarily discourage the opposition, then raced fifteen feet to the north and flattened at the base of a thicket, pressing flush with the vegetation.

Return fire was directed at the tree. Gunners converged on the run, seven of them in all, deriving courage from strength in numbers. The first three to reach the spot frantically searched the grass and weeds, one shouting angrily in Spanish. The hardmen spread out and advanced cautiously, conducting a sweep.

Bolan could only see a few of them. His body rigid, he watched as they moved deeper into the woods. One gunner passed within five feet of the thicket but failed to notice him. The crunch of their footsteps gradually receded, and when he was satisfied they were far enough away, the Executioner uncoiled and squatted. Keeping low, he raced to the road.

Flickering flames rose from the burning car, a charred body sprawled nearby. The crackling fire revealed not all the hardmen were in the woods.

The warrior froze at the sight of a single foe standing next to the Ford. A burly, bearded man had opened the rear door and was bent over Maria, slapping her on the face.

"Wake up, bitch."

Bolan closed in a blur. There was no time for finesse. He gripped the barrel and swung the rifle like a club, catching the bearded hardman in the face as the guy turned to confront him. Knocked into the door, the gunner clawed for a pistol on his right hip. Bolan swung again, smashing the stock onto the guy's forehead, dropping him to his knees. A third clubbing rendered him unconscious.

Closing the door, the warrior got behind the wheel and turned the engine over. He threw the Ford into Reverse and backed onto the road, then drove toward the second car. If he disposed of the other pursuit vehicle he'd be in the clear. His hand groped for the fourth fragmentation grenade, his fingers brushing its smooth surface at the same moment a pair of hardmen materialized in the trees on the left side of the road, assault rifles pressed to their shoulders. Ducking, he heard the chatter of their weapons and the pinging thuds of their rounds striking the side of the car. None penetrated his door, and in a heartbeat he was past them and coming even with the second pursuit vehicle. He used his teeth to pull the grenade's pin, then flipped the bomb out and glanced back to see it bounce and roll underneath their sedan. His foot wedged the accelerator to the floor.

He was barely out of range when a miniature sun blossomed in the rearview mirror and the pursuit vehicle exploded in flames.

Bolan raced to the intersection, glanced in all directions to see if there were other cars in sight, then took a right turn when he saw that all was clear.

By taking a winding, circuitous route, the warrior looped to the west and headed for Panama City. When he spied the lights of the metropolis, he found an isolated spot and pulled over. More than an hour had elapsed since he'd found Maria, and he wanted to try to revive her again. Leaving the hardware on the seat, except for the pistol, he got out and opened the back door.

Maria lay in shadow. She was on her left side, her right arm dangling to the floor, her dark hair concealing her face.

"Maria?" Bolan said softly, and placed his knee on the edge of the seat as he leaned inside. He gently shook her shoulder. "Maria, it's Mike. You're safe now."

She gave no sign of hearing.

Bolan brushed her hair aside and saw that her eyes were closed. The growl of a vehicle in the distance caused him to look up. He pinpointed the location as somewhere far to the northwest and traveling in the opposite direction.

"Maria, it's Mike," Bolan said, holding her steady. Her lips twitched, then parted to voice a barely audible croak.

"Mike?"

"Mike Belasko. I got you out."

Maria's eyes snapped wide. In a daze, she stared at him, her brow furrowed. "Mike?"

"Don't you remember me?"

Suddenly Maria did. She smiled wanly and tried to sit up.

"Don't exert yourself," Bolan cautioned. "You've been through hell. I have to get you to a doctor right away. I have a contact here who can arrange it."

Blinking, Maria looked around, then shuddered. "Oh, God. I thought I was done for."

A shudder racked Maria's body. She gasped, horror reflected in her countenance. "I remember it all! You have no idea what they did to me."

"Yes, I do. Try not to think about it."

"What they did," Maria repeated, as if she hadn't heard. "They pumped me full of drugs."

"I know."

Maria sniffled and spoke in a raspy whisper. "They abused me, did vile, despicable things to me."

"Shh. Don't talk about it right now." She began to cry, great uncontrollable sobs, her shoulders shaking. He sat out the emotional storm, caressing her hair, knowing there was nothing he could say to alleviate her misery. After a long while her crying tapered off and she mumbled a few words. "What?" he asked.

"You were right."

"About what?"

"About biting off more than I could chew. I should have listened to you. I'm sorry."

"You were doing what you thought was right."

"And I almost got myself killed."

"Listen to me," Bolan said gently. "You were justified in feeling the way you did. The loss of a loved one is hard enough to accept without having them die at the hands of those who prey on the innocent and the helpless. Believe me, I know." He paused. "If it's any consolation, I would have done the same thing if I was in your shoes."

"You would?"

"There are some things we can't turn our backs on and walk away as if nothing has happened."

"But now Espinosa and the others are free to do as they please."

"You don't have to worry about them."

"What are you planning to do?"

"I'll finish the job you started."

"Are you doing this for me?"

"For both of us."

"I don't understand."

"You don't have to."

Sitting up, Maria kissed him on the cheek. "I'll always be in your debt. How can I ever repay you?"

"By getting on with your life. You're tough, Maria. Use that toughness to bounce back. Forget about all of this and find some peace of mind."

"What about you, Mike? Do you ever know peace of mind? From that first day in my house, I've had the impression you're haunted by something in your past."

"My ghosts were put to rest a long time ago."

"Are you sure?"

Bolan didn't bother to answer. The sooner he saw her safely back to the States, the sooner he could get down to business. The time had come for Espinosa and Remón to pay the piper. They were long overdue for a taste of their own medicine, and he was going to give it to them.

Executioner style.

The jet skimmed over the treetops at a speed of six hundred miles per hour, leaving the blue expanse of sea behind and substituting a green canopy of unending jungle. Not thirty minutes ago the AV-8B Harrier took off from a carrier in the Caribbean Sea with Bolan's good friend and ace pilot Jack Grimaldi at the controls.

"Five minutes to the drop point, Striker," Grimaldi reported.

"Roger," Bolan replied mechanically, gazing at the lush landscape below revealed in the light from the rising sun. He was almost there, at last, and he couldn't wait to get his feet on Panamanian soil again.

Brognola had handled the arrangements for transporting Maria back to the States and booked her into a private hospital in the Miami area. Out of a sense of obligation, Bolan accompanied her the entire trip. He'd stayed at a nearby motel for two days and spent every minute of the allotted visiting time at her bedside.

The doctor in charge of her recovery was glad to have Bolan there. While the physician offered an excellent physical prognosis, he was concerned about Maria's mental and emotional state. Since she responded so positively to the big man and seemed happiest when Bolan visited, the doctor encouraged him to do so as often as possible.

Bolan stuck around as long as he could, then broke the news to Maria. She understood the necessity, but made him promise to visit her after the job was done.

Now that the Executioner was about to go to war again, he felt his anticipation rising. The whole time in Miami he'd been impatient to get back to Panama and attend to Remón and Espinosa. According to Brognola's sources, Remón cleared out of his estate after the rescue and went to his plantation deep in the interior. Whether Espinosa had accompanied him was unknown.

It was Brognola who had contacted Jack Grimaldi at the Stony Man Farm command post in Virginia's Blue Ridge Mountains and asked if the ace pilot would be interested in flying Bolan in. Naturally, considering the close friendship between the Executioner and the pilot, Grimaldi eagerly accepted.

The big Fed also set up the link to the carrier and provided the equipment Bolan requested for the clandestine mission. Besides camouflage fatigues and the usual complement of military webbing and pouches filled with garrotes, stilettos, ammo and assorted other weapons of war, he carried a Beretta, a Desert Eagle, a M-16A1 with an attached M-203 40 mm grenade launcher. In his lap rested a camouflage backpack containing his radio, binoculars, canteen, rations and the kicker, a special surprise he had in store for the drug lord.

Thanks to the informer, they knew Remón's plantation was situated in a high valley in the Serranía del Darien, close to the Colombian border. Although the informer didn't know the precise map coordinates, he did reveal the plantation was on the north bank of the Lindo, a minor tributary of the Chucunaque River, which narrowed down the search considerably. Brognola's cartographical experts isolated a ten-square-mile area where they felt the plantation might be.

A surprising question from Grimaldi interrupted Bolan's musing.

"You want any company on this one, Striker?"

"No, thanks, Jack, but I appreciate the offer."

"Are you sure? I wouldn't mind tagging along."

"Those Navy boys will have heart attacks if their V/STOL doesn't return on schedule."

"Let them wait. I don't mind."

Bolan stared at the back of Grimaldi's white helmet. "Maybe another time."

"Okay. Suit yourself."

The warrior twisted his neck to ease a kink, listening to the whine of the Harrier's Rolls-Royce Pegasus II turbofan engine, a power plant capable of delivering over twenty-one thousand pounds of thrust. With its vertical/short takeoff and landing ability, the jet didn't need to rely on runaways. Any road, grass field or small clearing was suitable.

Bolan checked his gear a final time. He wondered if Espinosa was still in Panama or back in the States.

Brognola's sources had no way of knowing, which didn't really matter because Bolan intended to track him down wherever he might be.

"One minute."

"I'm as ready as I'll ever be," Bolan replied.

The Harrier slowed and angled into a long valley running from north to south.

Bolan saw a stream and a pool at the base of a steep cliff, and then they were sweeping in over a wide grass-covered meadow. He felt the craft bank slightly and the thrust cut back even more.

"I'll set her down at the south edge if it's all right with you," Grimaldi stated.

"Looks fine."

With a precision few men could match, Grimaldi brought the Harrier down quickly and gently. He scanned the meadow, slid back the canopy and twisted in his seat to grin at Bolan. "End of the line, Striker. Time to kick some ass."

The warrior clapped his friend on the shoulder as he went down the boarding ladder. "Thanks, again," he called, and made for the jungle. No sooner did he drop to his knees to put on the backpack than the Harrier's engine roared and the V/STOL rose above the trees again. Through the branches he watched the gleaming aircraft swing to the east a few hundred feet, then streak off in the direction of the Caribbean Sea.

Bolan was alone in the primeval wilderness. After adjusting the backpack's straps to where they fit his shoulders snugly, he hefted the rifle and hiked to the south. If the experts were right, Remón's plantation lay somewhere along the flat land between the valley and the tributary of the Chucunaque. As a security precaution, Grimaldi had dropped him more than ten miles from the suspected site. Any closer, and someone at the plantation or living in the adjacent countryside might have spotted or heard the jet.

The warrior entered a vibrant domain that pulsed with the sights and sounds of countless creatures. Gaily plumed birds flew from tree to tree. Monkeys swung from limb to limb or chattered angrily at the alien intruder. A bewildering variety of insects, some the size of a man's hand, buzzed, chirped or flitted about. The familiar musty scent filled his nostrils, and the muggy air made his lungs work a bit harder to draw in each breath.

Bolan broke into a dogtrot and in no time at all was sweating profusely. He enjoyed the sensation of his body loosening up, his muscles becoming limber and relaxed. The backpack swished slightly as it rubbed against his shoulder blades. Fortunately—since he had so many miles to cover—the going was practically all downhill, a gradual descent that was evident only if one studied a map.

The warrior occasionally consulted his watch. After half an hour he stopped for a brief break and to get his bearings. He opened the backpack, took a swig from his canteen and swallowed a couple of salt tablets. He then aligned the pack on his back once more and headed out, the M-16 in his left hand. Twice he slowed to chop through a barrier of dense undergrowth, the razor-sharp machete slicing through wrist-thick vines and limbs with one stroke.

When the Executioner was within sight of the level expanse bordering the tributary, he stopped and trained the binoculars on the terrain. As he adjusted the magnification factor, a low growl sounded to his right. Glancing around, he discovered an animal had taken an interest in him.

Crouched twenty feet away at the base of a eucalyptus was a jaguar. The biggest and most powerful of cats found in the Western Hemisphere, they grew to lengths of eight feet and weighed as much as three hundred pounds. Indians feared them almost as much as they did the anaconda snake, although reports of attacks on humans were rare.

Bolan stood stock-still and waited for the animal to make a move. He didn't want to provoke it; by the same token he was confident the Desert Eagle could stop a charge, although he'd rather not use the gun this close to the presumed location of Remón's stronghold.

The jaguar rose after a minute, voiced a challenging snarl and bounded into the trees.

Watching the cat depart, Bolan thought about another jaguar, a killer far more sinister, the refined assassin who dispensed death as if practicing a fine art. Rarely did Bolan run into someone whose expertise matched or exceeded his own. The Jaguar was one of those exceptions. Twice they'd clashed and both had survived, but the next encounter promised to be the last for one of them.

Through the field glasses, Bolan saw stretches of the river on the horizon. Ahead were clusters of forest and tracts where high weeds flourished. Nowhere was there any sign of a plantation. Lifting the M-16, he headed out, planning to conduct a thorough sweep. The trail he followed had broadened, indicating regular use by large animals or man.

The sun climbed to its zenith, driving the temperature into the upper eighties. Bolan repeatedly mopped at his brow but refrained from drinking to conserve his water. Soon he came to a narrow plain that extended all the way to the tributary. Much nearer, and coming in his direction along the trail, were several people. He darted into the weeds and crouched.

Voices arose, a casual conversation punctuated by occasional laughter.

Bolan was reassured by the calm banter even though he'd never heard the language before. If they'd seen him, there would be shouts of alarm. Carefully parting the weeds, he peeked out at three Indians, two men and a woman.

All three were nearly naked, their skin bronzed by constant exposure to the sun. The men wore simple loincloths and carried long, thin spears. The woman wore a skimpy leather skirt around her middle, but her pendulous breasts bobbed freely as she walked. All three had dark hair and dark eyes.

The warrior let them go by. Establishing contact could jeopardize the mission. For all he knew, their tribe was on friendly terms with Harmodio Remón. To guarantee total secrecy and retain the element of surprise, he had to avoid the locals. He eased from cover when their voices faded and checked in both directions. Satisfied the trail was clear, he resumed his trek with heightened alertness.

The presence of the natives indicated there was a village in the area, which meant there were bound to be more Indians abroad. His best bet was to hole up until nightfall and conduct the search then. With that in mind he scoured the landscape for a suitable hiding place, his gaze roving to the southwest, and there, close to the Lindo, he found the plantation.

19

Amazingly, or perhaps because Remón had important government and military officials in the financial palm of his hand, no effort was made to conceal the high-grade sinsemilla marijuana growing on two hundred acres surrounding the palatial house and walled grounds. Robust marijuana stalks, some seven and eight feet high, formed a sea of dark green at the edge of the plain, bordering the Lindo. Scores of workers, the majority Indians, worked at cultivating the plants and removing weeds.

The heart of the plantation was the twenty-acre plot on which stood the house and other buildings that were partially visible above the high white wall. A wide gate afforded access to the grounds, and a dirt road connected the estate to a dock on the Lindo. Between the south wall and the river was a narrow airstrip where two planes were parked.

Bolan took all of this in as he made his way through the marijuana fields toward the north wall. The Indian workers went about their tasks methodically and seldom lifted their heads from their jobs, which made getting past them easier than the warrior expected. His camouflage fatigues blended in perfectly with the plants.

It took him the better part of two hours to work his way to within forty yards of the wall, and then he cautiously moved around to the west where he could see the gate more clearly. He flattened and put his binoculars to good use, discovering a huge shed and what appeared to be a barracks. There were people everywhere, the majority Indians, but there were also twenty or thirty hardmen strolling about with submachine guns or assault rifles slung over their shoulders.

Bolan didn't dare risk a penetration until nightfall. He occupied his time by taking in all the little details he could and monitoring the guards. A pair of gunners were stationed at the gate, and whenever an Indian left the compound they would search the native carefully, although in most cases the Indians wore nothing but loincloths or skirts like those Bolan had seen earlier. He guessed the natives had to be pilfering things, perhaps tools or knives, and wondered if the mistrust was mutual.

Not until five o'clock did an unusual event take place. Antonio Espinosa, the Jaguar and a man who could only be Harmodio Remón left the house and went to the shed.

The warrior fixed the binoculars on the trio and saw Espinosa talking a mile a minute to Remón, who was a short, stocky man with curly gray hair and a drooping mustache. Behind them, alertly taking in all that went on, walked the Jaguar.

Bolan watched them enter the shed. He could nail them when they came out, but for an unobstructed shot he'd need to stand fully erect and expose himself to the guards. Better to wait, he reasoned, and eliminate them with his surprise package in the backpack.

Remón, Espinosa and the Jaguar emerged from the shed twenty minutes later. The Panamanian drug lord and his American guest were joking and laughing, the best of buddies.

Bolan wondered why Espinosa had remained in Panama. Obviously the pair had cemented whatever business arrangements needed to be worked out. Perhaps Remón was showing Espinosa his operation, impressing him with his power and efficiency. They were birds of a feather, vultures who preyed on the weak and the gullible, men who found pleasure in inflicting misery and pain on others, and as such they deserved the same fate.

The Executioner settled down for the long wait, lying at the base of several marijuana plants, invisible unless a worker stumbled right on top of him. The hours went by slowly. Insects buzzed in the field, and occasionally snatches of conversation drifted his way from clusters of Indians engaged in various labors.

Bolan was a supremely patient man. He could lie immobile for hours on end, if necessary, and had done so on many an occasion in Vietnam when on extermination missions deep in Vietcong territory, and later when staking out possible Mafia targets. As with the big cat he'd seen in the jungle, patience was the key to a successful hunt. If a jaguar burst from cover before its prey was close enough to catch, it went hungry. If he tried to rush a shot or made a premature move, Bolan risked blowing everything.

Eventually the sun touched the western horizon. In small groups the Indians drifted in from the fields, many carrying hoes, shovels and other tools.

Bolan stayed low as the natives trudged past. None came close enough to spot him. They all were weary from their day's exertion and walked with bowed shoulders and tired strides. He imagined Remón paid them peanuts. They were a source of cheap, hard-working labor that the drug lord would exploit to the maximum.

Shortly after the last of the Indians quit the fields, they departed toward their village in a body, carrying their long spears, heading to the northeast.

Lights came on in the house and other buildings, and floodlights mounted on the walls flared to life. Surprisingly the gate stayed open.

As the sun dipped from sight and night enveloped the plantation, Bolan crept closer to the wall. Six feet from the last row of plants he halted and rechecked his gear and weapons. All was in readiness for the penetration.

He drew the Beretta and inched nearer, his eyes on the gate guards. He stopped again when he heard engines turning over and upraised voices. Puzzled, he saw the guards step to one side and stare into the compound.

An explanation was forthcoming a minute later when three trucks drove out and headed down the road toward the airstrip and the dock. Four Jeeps, loaded with gunners, followed. In the first Jeep rode Remón and the Jaguar.

Bolan gazed at the retreating taillights and came to the conclusion that Remón was either expecting a shipment of cocaine from the suppliers in Colombia or was getting set to send cocaine or marijuana out. Whatever the case, it meant most of the hardmen would be occupied for an hour or two. How convenient.

The warrior glided to the edge of the field and squatted. Both guards were smoking and chatting to the left of the gate, one man with his back to the field and the other in front of him so that the first man blocked his companion's view of the field. Bolan slung the rifle over his left shoulder, and with the Beretta in his right hand he moved from concealment, staying bent at the waist. Silently he closed, his finger on the trigger, listening to their idle discussion in Spanish, until he was a yard behind the first man. Sensing the warrior's presence, the man whirled.

Bolan fired a slug into the man's forehead at point-blank range, shifted his stance a fraction and placed his second shot into the center of the other guard's heart.

The two hardmen dropped soundlessly.

Quickly Bolan took hold of one guard and dragged him into the field, then returned for the other. Not a soul appeared to challenge him. He jogged to the gate and peered inside at a seemingly deserted compound. The house sat straight back from the gate. To the right was the shed, to the left the barracks. There were no gunners in sight.

Holstering the Beretta, Bolan unslung the M-16 and sprinted to the side of the shed. He stepped to a window and peered inside. Evidently Remón wasn't satisfied with letting nature take its course, because tons of chemical fertilizer occupied the south half of the structure. Crates and boxes were piled in the middle, while the remaining floor space was devoted to long tables and the equipment used in processing cocaine and marijuana.

The shed was empty.

The warrior slipped into the building and crouched behind the crates. He removed his backpack, opened the flap and removed one of the packets of C-4 plastic explosive. Concealing it in a space between two large crates, he set it up to detonate electrically. A second packet was strategically stashed in the middle of the stored chemical fertilizer.

Satisfied with his handiwork, the Executioner retrieved the backpack and left. He spied a garage in the southeast corner. Two more trucks were parked beside it, and he jogged over to apply C-4 to the gas tank of each.

Next came the barracks, which he circled cautiously before setting to work. There were five hardmen playing cards at a table at the rear, and dozens of empty cots lined along both walls. A packet was placed at each end of the building.

Leaving just the house.

Bolan worked his way around to the back, looking into several windows along the way. A few were open. He heard a radio playing, and as he neared the last window on the north side he heard someone speaking in English. The voice was vaguely familiar, but not until he was almost to the sill did he recognize it.

The speaker was Antonio Espinosa.

Stepping lightly forward, the big man peeked inside and discovered a communications room complete with sophisticated shortwave equipment. A Panamanian radio operator sat in a chair, smoking a cigarette and gazing up at the ceiling while waiting for Espinosa to finish.

The drug lord was hunched over a microphone. He wore a headset, and a smug grin creased his face as he nodded a few times. "Yeah, that's right, Nick. Two more days and I'm out of here. Is everything all set up?" He paused, listening to the response. "Perfect. I knew I could count on you. Just be sure they understand we're talking about three times the volume. If they can't hack it, I'll find someone who can."

Bolan slid under the window.

"Yeah. Yeah. The man has his act together. Working with him is the smartest move I've ever made. The DEA did me a favor by forcing me to fly down here," Espinosa went on. "I can't wait. A welcome home party is a great idea. See you then. And don't forget..."

The voice trailed off as Bolan reached a corner. Four packets remained in his backpack, and he planted one on each side of the house, doing the south side last. As he checked the detonator, he heard the front door open and close. He hugged the grass and crawled into the deepest shadows, dragging the backpack after him.

Espinosa appeared and walked toward the shed, whistling happily, his hands in his pockets.

What was this action? Bolan wondered as he followed the drug lord. A quick look in the window revealed the reason for Espinosa's good mood.

He'd removed the lid from one of the crates. He gazed into it, laughed heartily, then leaned down and took out a packaged kilo of coke. As if caressing a lover, Espinosa ran his hands over the key and kissed it.

Ducking beneath the window frame, Bolan slid the detonator into a front pocket, secured the backpack and shouldered it, and with the M-16 in his left hand catfooted to the front door. A survey of the grounds disclosed no opposition. Drawing the Beretta, he inched the door a crack and saw Espinosa replacing the crate lid.

The warrior stepped boldly into the shed and closed the door.

Not expecting trouble, Espinosa casually looked up, did a double-take and took a stride back. "You!" he blurted.

"Me," Bolan said, leveling the Beretta.

Espinosa extended his arms, palms outward. "Wait, man!" he pleaded. "We can make a deal!"

"I don't think so," Bolan replied, about to stroke the trigger when the partially open crate sparked an idea. He lowered the barrel slightly. "Take out a key."

"What?"

"Take out a kilo of coke."

Fumbling with the lid, Espinosa lifted a package and wagged it back and forth. "Here, man. You want one, it's yours. Take ten. Take all you can carry."

Bolan thought of Maria Salvato, of the murder of her son, of the harrowing ordeal she'd experienced, of her suffering and sorrow, of the lingering terror mirrored in her eyes after her rescue, and pronounced a two-word death sentence. "Eat it."

Espinosa blinked. "What?"

"Eat the coke."

Comprehension dawned. "No way."

"Suit yourself." Bolan shrugged and aimed.

"Wait!" Espinosa glanced from the pistol to the kilo and back again, weighing his choices. Instant death or a minute or two of life. He chose to cling to life. "I'll do it."

"Now."

The steely command prompted Espinosa to claw at the wrapping, his fingers straining while his eyes darted every which way, desperately seeking a means of turning the tables. Finally he succeeded in splitting the package, and white powder spilled out over his hands and wrists. Hesitating, he looked at his executioner and tried one last time. "I'm a rich man. I can give you all the money you'd ever want."

"Eat."

Espinosa nervously licked his lips, then dipped his fingers into the kilo and deposited a small amount of coke on the tip of his tongue.

"More," Bolan said.

Espinosa swallowed and shuddered. He upended a handful into his right palm, looked at the Beretta and crammed the cocaine into his mouth, sputtering and gagging as he did. Groaning, he downed the drug and groaned. Tears filled his eyes and spittle dripped from his lips.

"Keep going," the warrior directed.

Espinosa frowned, then squared his shoulders defiantly, suddenly finding his backbone. "This is shit! Tony Espinosa doesn't kiss anyone's ass." He lunged for a crowbar next to the crate.

"This is for Maria Salvato." A pair of holes blossomed on Espinosa's chest, and he sank to the floor in a twisting spiral.

Bolan heard the rumble of trucks in the distance. Pivoting, he walked to the door. The noise of the returning convoy indicated the vehicles weren't far from the gate. He didn't have much time to get into position for the final confrontation with the forces of Harmodio Remón. Holstering the Beretta once again, he grasped the M-16 and raced into the night.

20

The Executioner was halfway to the gate when he saw headlight beams play over the ground beyond. Swerving, he sprinted to the west wall and dropped prone in the shadow at its base, facing the entrance with the M-16 pressed to his right shoulder.

Seconds later the convoy returned. This time the four Jeeps were in the lead. They braked abruptly just inside the entrance and Harmodio Remón glanced in both directions, evidently looking for the missing guards. He barked a word to the driver. The Jeeps drove up to the front of the house and stopped. The three trucks angled to the front of the shed.

So far no one had spotted him, but Bolan knew his luck wouldn't hold forever. Since he wanted to be outside the walls when he detonated the plastique, a diversion was called for, something to keep the hardmen occupied while he made his getaway. He had just the thing.

The warrior yanked an orange high-explosive round from his webbing and fed it into the grenade launcher. The armor-piercing round could penetrate two inches of steel. Sighting on the lead truck, he let the can fly and hugged the ground.

The grenade hit behind the cab and buckled the vehicle, wiping out the driver and another gunner in the bargain, in a thunderous burst amplified by the walls and buildings.

Cries of alarm and curses filled the air as Bolan sent another grenade into the second truck's cab.

Shouts of confusion were voiced by hardmen spilling from every vehicle. The men from the barracks ran out to help, looking in all directions for the attacking party.

Too many gunners were milling about for Bolan to risk a sprint to the gate. To reduce the odds, he selected a light gold projectile, an airburst grenade, his fingers flying, and delivered the round in the center of a group of confused hardmen. The bounding fragmentation grenade struck the grass, then arced about five feet into the air before going off. Five bodies littered the ground when the echoes died.

Someone bellowed orders, trying to organize resistance. Above the din a shrill voice shrieked, "Where the hell is it coming from?"

Bolan wasn't telling. He reverted to a smoke hand grenade, throwing in an overhand toss and planting it near the truck. A second grenade landed a dozen yards from the barracks. Both immediately spewed thick white smoke over the lawn, providing a vaporous screen between the gunners and the gate.

Pushing himself erect, the warrior pounded toward the opening. He spotted a vague form charging through the smoke and snapped off half a dozen rounds as a permanent deterrent. The form toppled soundlessly.

By now, Bolan calculated, Remón had to be taking cover in the house. Drug czars of Remón's stature rarely participated in pitched battles, not when they paid good money to gunners who were expected to do their fighting for them. Those at the top seldom jeopardized their lives, not to mention their opulent lifestyles, on the front lines.

Several hardmen opened fire, but none of the rounds went anywherc near the Executioner. He reached the gate, turned the corner and pulled the detonator from his pocket. Time for the big bang.

Bolan keyed the detonator and braced his legs for the shock.

With a precision only a demolition expert could achieve, the packets of plastique went off within twenty to thirty milliseconds of each other, a series of deafening explosions rocking the compound. The shed went first, shooting a billowing fireball toward the moon and illuminating the immediate area.

The ground shook violently, and concussive waves struck the wall, shaking it to its foundation. The tortured grinding of twisted metal, the screams of dying men and tremendous crashing sounds formed a chorus of destruction.

Bolan weathered the explosions, then slid a buckshot canister into the M-203 and moved to the gate. A quick peek verified torn and ruptured figures sprawled in gruesome attitudes of death. All three trucks were so much slag, and three of the Jeeps were in flames. Amazingly, the fourth Jeep was untouched.

Little remained of the shed except a burning square of galvanized scrap metal. Both ends of the barracks were shattered skeletons of charred wood. The house, where he'd set up most of the charges, had lost all of its windows and two of its walls, and was burning furiously. Clouds of smoke hovered at ground level, partially obscuring portions of the lawn.

Advancing carefully, the Executioner spotted a shooter off to the left who appeared to be in a state of shock. Mechanically the man clawed for a pistol, and Bolan drilled a fist-size pattern of shots into the guy's chest.

A pair of coughing, staggering hardmen, both unarmed, stumbled into view on the right. Their clothes were torn, their faces grimy. They took one look at the steely apparition in front of them and halted.

Bolan covered them, letting them decide whether they lived or died.

One of the hardmen held out his empty hands, wheezed and shook his head. "No more, man," he pleaded. "We've had enough."

Jerking his thumb at the gate, the warrior motioned for them to leave and they complied with remarkable speed. He went on, seeking Remón's remains, wanting to be sure. He jogged to the Jeep, noticed a set of keys dangling from the ignition and stepped as close as he dared to the house. Intense heat from the crackling flames drove him back. There were bodies all around, most burned beyond recognition.

He scanned them, hoping to spot Remón, desiring confirmation, but realized identifying the drug lord was a hopeless task.

Turning, the warrior surveyed the grounds. Nothing moved in the midst of the carnage. A troubling doubt gnawed at the back of his mind. Had he taken out all of Remón's troops? He wished he'd been able to make an accurate tally before the fight. As it was, with so many hardmen blown to bits or nearly incinerated, making an accurate body count was impossible. Since no more gunners had appeared, it seemed obvious he'd eliminated all of them.

Still, something bothered him.

Bolan stepped to the undamaged Jeep. Before radioing Grimaldi, a check of the airstrip and the dock was in order. Any drugs awaiting shipment at either place had to be destroyed. As he started to slide behind the steering wheel, he glanced at the northeast corner of the property and spied several figures going over the wall.

Some of the hardmen were escaping. Or did they plan to work their way around and get him in the back? He could let them go, but he didn't like the idea of having armed gunners somewhere in the area while he mopped up. Better to be safe than sorry. Removing a fresh magazine from a utility pouch, he depressed the magazine release button, pulled the partially spent magazine straight down and tossed it aside, then inserted the full one and took off toward the corner.

Bolan covered the ground swiftly. He found two large trash barrels had been flipped over and placed next to the wall at the point where the hardmen went over, and it took but seconds to climb on top of the nearest. Straining his ears, he failed to detect any sounds that indicated the gunners were lurking on the far side. The M-16 went over his left shoulder. He crouched, then vaulted upward, his outstretched hands easily grasping the rim. His momentum brought him high enough to prop both elbows on top, and he paused to stare at the marijuana field.

Four men were fleeing northward.

The warrior almost let them go. He started to lower himself down to the trash barrel when one of the men looked back. Although the distance was too great to distinguish the man's features clearly, and although the marijuana plants obscured parts of the man's body, Bolan believed he knew who it was.

Harmodio Remón.

Surging up and over the wall, the big man landed lightly and gave chase, unslinging the rifle as he sped between two rows of six-foot-high plants. He might be mistaken but he couldn't take the chance. Without Remón dead, the mission was a bust. The drug lord could have made for the wall at any point, probably once he saw his men being annihilated and before the shed went up.

To conserve his strength, the warrior maintained a steady pace instead of running all out. At ground level his quarry was intermittently visible, heading in a beeline for the jungle. They were bound to beat him there, which didn't bother Bolan a bit. The jungle was his element. He'd have the advantage.

The warrior stopped regularly to probe the night for hint of an ambush. He didn't know if the quartet knew he was in pursuit, but caution dictated he act under the assumption they did. Conclusive proof came when he was two-thirds of the way across the field.

Three rounds blasted out of the night to smack into a marijuana plant on the big man's right.

Bolan instinctively hit the dirt, then scrambled to the left into the next row. He knew he was alive because the sniper rushed the shots. On his hands and knees he worked his way over three more rows, then crawled in the direction the shots came from.

A test of nerves and stealth ensued. Bolan kept his eyes at ground level, seeking the telltale flicker of movement. If the sniper had any smarts he'd be doing the same thing.

The warrior held the M-16 in front of his body. A large insect scuttled across his right hand and he ignored it. After crawling for a minute he spied the sniper; a hunched-over figure was moving from plant to plant approximately fifteen yards northeast of his position.

Bolan sighted on the hardman, tracking his furtive movements. There wouldn't be a clear shot thanks to all the stalks and leaves. He counted the steps the man took and discovered a pattern of two quick strides to each marijuana plant, a pause while the sniper stood behind the stalk, then two more strides to the next one. He waited until the man paused, and the instant the sniper stepped out the Executioner banged off three shots.

Knocked backward, the man stumbled over a plant and went down on his side. He tried to rise, managed to get to his knees, then collapsed.

Wary of a trick, Bolan advanced cautiously, the M-16 trained on the hardman all the while. He needn't have worried. His rounds had perforated the guy's chest near his heart.

Now there were three left, counting Remón.

The warrior stayed low and moved rapidly to the end of the field, where a narrow strip of clear ground separated the marijuana plantation from the jungle. He'd be a perfect target in the seconds required to cross it. Kneeling behind a stalk, he scanned the wall of vegetation, concentrating on the trunks of trees.

If Bolan read Remón's game plan correctly, there had to be a gunner in there. The drug lord was sacrificing his pawns to check the warrior's pursuit, apparently buying time to get...where? Did Remón intend to swing around the estate and escape in a plane or boat? Or was there an ulterior motive?

A flicker of movement and the dull glint of moonlight off metal gave away the presence of a gunner crouched at the base of a mahogany tree to the east.

Another game of cat and mouse would delay Bolan too long. He selected a short black canister from his belt and slid it into the M-203. A buckshot grenade was ideal for jungle environments and where poor visibility made targets elusive. Like buckshot from a shotgun, it produced a wide killing pattern in a limited space. Peering through the sight leaf, he remembered to aim at the base of the tree instead of allowing for a trajectory. Unlike high-explosive and airburst grenades, buckshot projectiles had a high muzzle velocity. This one demonstrated as much by striking exactly the point he aimed at.

A bright burst, a strangled scream, and the shredded gunner was no longer a threat.

Relying on the explosion to distract anyone else who might be lurking in the nearby jungle, the Executioner sprinted into the trees and ducked behind one. As far as he knew, only one gunner and Remón remained alive. After the battle at the plantation, such odds seemed insignificant. But all it took was one bullet to end his life, and even the lowliest, most bumbling amateur could get lucky.

Bolan scanned the jungle repeatedly. The grenade had silenced the insects and other wildlife, shrouding the thick vegetation in deathly stillness. Only when he was completely satisfied there were no hardmen waiting in ambush did Bolan move northward again.

He skirted a dense clump of shoulder-high bushes, his soft soles making no noise, the perfect soldier at home in the perfect predatory environment. The moon's pale light gave the landscape an eerie whitish glow, making the leaves, limbs and vines seem as if they were lighted from within by an unearthly source.

Bolan stayed on the same bearing, trusting in his instincts to warn him of danger. He bisected a narrow trail running from the southwest to the northeast, and hesitated.

Acting on a hunch, Bolan took the trail, heading northeast. Walls of undergrowth on both sides hemmed him in. Several times he passed under large branches. An unusual object lying in the grass on the right side and jutting into the path caught his attention, and he paused to check it out. Squatting, he discovered a broken stone ax of the type typically carried by Indian warriors, and suddenly he realized where Remón was going.

Rising, the warrior ran all out, hoping he'd catch up to the drug lord before Remón reached the village. He had to assume Remón would ask the Indians for help, probably feeding them a lie about Bolan being a bad man who would destroy them. The Indians, not knowing any better, would try to hunt him down. And the last thing he needed was scores of Indians on his trail. They were innocents, and he refused to fight them except in self-defense.

If Remón reached the village, Bolan knew he'd have no choice but to abort the mission and head for the rendezvous point. As much as he hated to leave a job unfinished, he had no desire to try to evade the best trackers and hunters in existence. His gaze flicked over the trail, alert for another ambush or sight of the village. He passed underneath a leafy limb and thought nothing of it until he heard a scratching sound and felt a heavy body slam into his back.

21

If not for the backpack, the blow would have broken Bolan's spine. He went down hard on his hands and knees, intentionally letting go of the M-16, then threw himself to the left and grabbed for the Desert Eagle even though he knew he was too late. The pressure of a gun barrel against his temple proved him right, and he braced for the shot that, inexplicably, never came.

"Not a move, amigo, not so much as a twitch, eh?"

Bolan recognized the voice. He stayed rigid as the lean man in black stepped around in front of him, grinning smugly.

"We meet again, Belasko," the Jaguar said. Clutched in his left hand was a Browning Hi-Power pistol. "Although I doubt Belasko is your real name."

The warrior didn't bother to respond. He concentrated on keeping his mind sharp and being ready for the first opportunity that presented itself. For some reason the Jaguar wanted him alive, a situation he might be able to exploit.

"We will do this by the numbers, Señor Belasko," the Jaguar stated. "First you will sit up and put your hands behind your head. Do so slowly or you will lose that head.''

Bolan complied.

"Excellent. You are a reasonable man, which is to be expected of someone of your caliber. So many of the young ones are too rash for their own good. They make stupid mistakes and pay with their lives. Would you agree?''

Bolan kept silent.

"It won't kill you to talk," the Jaguar said, and chuckled. He slowly moved behind the warrior, the Browning held steady. "Please stay still or I will be forced to shoot you.''

A hand slid under Bolan's arm and plucked the Beretta from its holster. A second later the Desert Eagle was taken. He watched the deadly figure step into view again on his left. The Jaguar tossed the handguns to the side of the trail, then did the same with the M-16.

"So much for temptation.''

The Jaguar positioned himself five feet in front of the big man and squatted. "Are you ready to talk yet?''

Bolan saw no reason to continue the silence. "What do we have to talk about?''

"Your curiosity, perhaps.''

"In what respect?''

"Come now," the Jaguar said, and laughed lightly. "If I was in your shoes, I would be intensely curious as to why I was still alive. Aren't you?''

"The thought did cross my mind.''

"Of course it did. To tell the truth, if the decision had been mine I would have killed you with a single shot to the head. You do agree I could have done so?"

The warrior nodded curtly.

"Which is not easy to do when dealing with a man as competent as yourself," the Jaguar remarked.

Bolan listened attentively, mystified by the killer's behavior, by all the flattery and the Jaguar's nonchalant attitude. Of all the hit men, assassins and shooters he'd ever met, this man was unique.

"You owe your life to Harmodio."

"I do?"

"Yes. He requested that I try to take you alive. I had my doubts such a feat was possible, but I liked the challenge. You are not a man to be taken lightly."

"And when Remón snaps his fingers, you jump," Bolan said.

"Whatever Harmodio wants, I do. You would do no less for *your* brother."

The revelation surprised Bolan, although it shouldn't have. He'd suspected there was more to their relationship than met the eye; he just never figured they were related. It explained a lot. Like why the Jaguar worked exclusively for Harmodio. Like why Harmodio trusted the Jaguar implicitly. And why the Jaguar functioned more as a second in command instead of merely a professional killer.

"I knew we would meet again."

"You did?" Bolan said simply to hold up his end of the conversation. Stay sharp, he kept telling himself.

"Certainly. You might call it an instinct I have about such matters. Besides, I never saw your body back in Miami, and I learned long ago never to take it for granted the opposition has been eliminated until I have touched the corpse with my own hands. I would imagine you are equally as prudent."

"Not prudent enough, it seems."

The Jaguar grinned. "I like you, Belasko. Most of those in our profession have no sense of humor. They're more like machines than men. I find them such bores."

Bolan relaxed his arms. He still had the Ka-bar and two stilettos. If he could only get his hands on one of the blades, he stood an even chance of turning the tables on his overconfident captor.

"We heard about the two men you stuffed down the laundry chute at your hotel," the Jaguar said. "You must be wondering how we learned you were in the country so quickly?"

"How did you?" Bolan asked, although he already knew.

"We monitor all incoming and outgoing flights to make sure we don't receive any nasty surprises. I added your name to a list of those our men should watch out for. When they called and told us you were in the country, Harmodio ordered them to take you out." The Jaguar sighed. "I would have preferred to do the job myself, but he insisted I stay by his side."

"Where is your brother now?"

"Oh. That's right. I have not told you yet."

"Told me what?"

"The reason Harmodio wants you alive. He went to get the Teremembes."

"The Indians?"

"Yes. As you no doubt noticed, they work our plantation in exchange for food, tools, a few weapons and worthless trinkets. It is an excellent business arrangement and increased our profit margin substantially."

"I can imagine."

"The Teremembes are such children. Show them a few kindnesses and they are your friends for life. And there are many more tribes just like them. The last I heard, there are more than 50,000 Indians living in remote regions of Panama, living much as their ancestors did by hunting, fishing and trapping.

"They are like children, but very deadly children," the Jaguar went on, gazing past the big man along the trail to the northeast. "They conduct raids on each other all the time. The fat *politicos* can pass all the laws they want, and the priests can preach until they are blue in the face, but they will never change the natives."

Bolan detected a note of pride, even affection, when the Jaguar talked about the Indians. "You sound very fond of them."

"*Sí.* I spent a year living among the Teremembes when I was fifteen. Part of my training."

"Training?"

"Harmodio saw to it. In order that I might become the perfect assassin, he spared no expense and effort in having me trained by the best in the business. I

learned jungle survival and other skills from the Teremembes.''

More mysteries were cleared up. Now Bolan knew
how the Jaguar could move so silently and skillfully
and why the younger Remón was one of the most
feared assassins on the globe.

"The Teremembes are also masters at torture. I've
seen them skin a man alive. And they inflict such exquisite torment with bamboo slivers that their victims
beg to be put out of their misery.''

Bolan said nothing. He simply waited.

"In fact, you will soon experience such things for
yourself. Harmodio and the Teremembes should be
here any minute.''

The warrior listened but heard nothing.

"Harmodio wanted me to take you alive so he can
watch them reduce you to a quivering mass of flesh.
It's his way of getting revenge for what you've done to
his operation.'' The Jaguar snickered. "I have never
seen him so mad as he was tonight. It was all I could
do to drag him from the plantation. He wanted to tear
into you himself.''

"You should have let him.''

The Jaguar rubbed the back of his neck and looked
down the trail again. "Harmodio would not stand a
prayer against a man like you. He's not in our class in
that respect.''

"Your brother is scum.''

Those cold green eyes locked on the warrior's face
and narrowed. For a few moments the Jaguar studied
Bolan, then smiled. "I see what you are trying to do.

Get me angry and I'll make a mistake, let you grab my gun perhaps? Really, Belasko. Do you think I am that gullible?''

"You can't fault a man for trying."

"True. But I expect to be treated with more respect, the same respect I have accorded you. It's so rare for me to encounter anyone who rivals my skills. This is a treat."

"Glad I could make your day."

The Jaguar slowly straightened and focused on the trail. "I hope Harmodio reached the village safely," he said, more to himself than the warrior. "There are many dangerous animals roaming the jungle at night."

At last. Bolan saw a way to increase his odds. "Yeah. I know," he said. "I bumped into the biggest snake I've ever seen not far from here."

"You did?"

"Don't know what kind it was. Probably a boa from the size of it." Bolan paused. "How big do they grow, anyway?"

"I saw a boa twenty feet long once," the Jaguar said, still looking at the trail. "And the anacondas, of course, grow much, much larger."

"I wouldn't want to stumble onto one of those things in the dark," Bolan commented. "I bet they can crush a man to a pulp in seconds." He saw the Jaguar's lips compress, could almost see the gears turning, and was pleased to note a flicker of worry etch the killer's face.

"Stand up."

Bolan feigned surprise. "What?"

"You heard me. Stand up. Keep your hands behind your head at all times."

The warrior complied.

"Now turn and march. Stay in the middle of the trail."

Bolan did as he was told, wishing he could devise a way of discarding his backpack. The extra weight and bulk, however marginal, would impede his movements when the time came. "Where are we going?"

"Where do you think? We'll meet Harmodio on the trail or walk all the way to the Teremembes' village if necessary."

Now came the hard part. First Bolan needed to know the exact distance separating the two of them. He listened to the wildlife sounds, biding his time. Even at night the jungle was alive with the cries of predators and the prey they hunted. When a loud squawk issued from the trees on the right, perhaps made by a startled parrot, he used the noise as an excuse to twist his neck and glance in that direction. Out of the corner of his eye he noted the Jaguar's position, a yard behind him, and faced front.

"What is your real name, Belasko?"

The unexpected question gave Bolan an excuse to slow slightly. "Does it matter?"

"It would be nice to know the name of the hombre who has given me more trouble than any other man."

"Belasko will do."

"As you wish. But I should warn you that whatever you fail to tell me now will be pried from your lips by the Teremembes. They have marvelous ways of making a person talk. By the time they are done, I will know all there is to know about you."

Bolan concentrated on the animal noises, hoping for the right one.

"You will also tell us the identity of your employer."

"I'm not working for anyone."

"Please don't insult my intelligence. A man like you does not take on someone like Harmodio for the hell of it, especially when you must have known I am his main enforcer."

The egotism again. Bolan had never met a killer as vain as the younger Remón. He derailed the train of thought, keeping his mind clear for the right moment, which came sooner than he expected.

From the dense undergrowth to the northwest, from only a few dozen yards away, came the fierce, throaty snarl of a jaguar.

22

Anyone who heard the snarl of so fierce a predator at such close range was bound to glance in the direction from which the sound came. The reaction would be automatic. Or so Bolan hoped as he spun and sprang, his arms extended, knowing all too well his life was on the line if he'd miscalculated.

But the Jaguar had involuntarily paused and looked to the northwest, a mere twist of the neck that diverted his attention from the warrior for all of one second. Movement registered in the corner of his eye and he realized his mistake. He tried to compensate by angling the Browning at the prisoner and squeezing the trigger.

Bolan went for the gun first, his left hand slashing into the Jaguar's wrist the same instant the pistol boomed, deflecting the gun arm aside a few inches. The bullet narrowly missed his chest and smacked into the ground.

Already the Jaguar was throwing himself to the right.

The warrior went with the movement, closing in, his left hand clamping on the killer's wrist as he drove his right knee up and into the groin area. But the Jaguar deftly turned his legs, just a hair, enough to take the brunt of the blow on the inner thigh, and their combined momentum carried them to the ground.

Bolan landed on his left side, retaining his grip on the assassin's wrist with an effort, and with his other hand snapped a palm-heel thrust at the Jaguar's chin. The wiry man in black jerked his head out of the way and retaliated with a karate blow, a punch delivered with the middle finger extended and rigid. Bolan tried to evade it, but the knuckles struck him a glancing blow on the jaw. He grabbed the other wrist and they rolled and thrashed, the Jaguar striving to break free and the warrior pounding the gun hand on the ground in an attempt to dislodge the weapon.

Both men rolled from the trail and into the undergrowth.

Bolan had no idea they were near a tree until they smacked into the trunk with a jarring impact. He rammed the gun arm against the bole twice in swift succession, and on the second try the Browning went flying. A knee slammed into his ribs, lancing agony through his torso and causing his grip to slacken.

In a flash the Jaguar was on his feet and backpedaling, giving himself room to maneuver.

As the warrior rose he saw the other adopt a back stance.

"Clever move, Belasko," the Jaguar said without a trace of malice. "Now let's see how good you really are."

Bolan moved slowly forward, and for every step he took the killer did the same backward. The Jaguar backed onto the trail and halted.

"I'm waiting, Belasko."

Bolan wondered why the enforcer was baiting him instead of getting down to business.

From nearby came the sounds of shouting, screeching and savage whooping.

The Jaguar smiled.

Suddenly Bolan understood. The assassin was stalling until the Teremembes arrived, and from the sound of things the Indians would be there in a few minutes.

"Do you hear that?" the Jaguar asked, smirking. "My brother will be here soon, and by tomorrow afternoon your hide will be drying in the sun."

The warrior had to end the impasse, and do it quickly. Fleeing into the jungle was out of the question. Without his guns he stood little chance against an entire tribe, and the Jaguar would probably trail him and give away his location to the Indians, anyway. He could duck into the undergrowth and try to take out the Jaguar with a grenade, but he doubted the assassin would stand still and let himself be blown to bits. No, the only way out was to promptly dispose of the man in black. With the decision came action, and he stripped off his backpack as he stepped cautiously toward his nemesis.

The Jaguar stood his ground, unfazed. He flicked his right wrist and out popped the double-edged, foot-long blade. "Give it up, Belasko. Make it easy on yourself."

Bolan didn't bother responding. He held the backpack in front of his body, screening his torso, and palmed a stiletto. The natives' whoops were growing louder. He figured he had three minutes, tops.

Holding the blade in a defensive posture, the Jaguar backed up another pace, his mocking expression gone, replaced by intense concentration.

Extending the backpack like a shield, the Executioner charged. He held the stiletto close to his abdomen, intending to go for the Jaguar's gut when the killer stabbed at the pack. Instead the man in black skipped to the left and crouched, arcing the long blade at Bolan's legs.

The warrior swerved and felt the razor tip slice into his pants, cutting the fabric and nicking his flesh. He evaded a second swipe, forced to retreat a yard to do so, and blocked a third with the pack.

A feral sneer creased the Jaguar's thin lips as he pressed his attack, taking advantage of his longer weapon, slashing and swiping over and over again, his swings precise, controlled, trying for a crippling stroke, not a lethal one.

It was all Bolan could do to avoid the glittering blade. The Jaguar's speed was exceptional, almost uncanny; he slit open the backpack in a dozen spots and made a four-inch tear in Bolan's shirtsleeve.

All the while the Teremembes were getting closer.

Bolan countered another stab with the pack, and tried a desperate gambit. There was no more time to lose. It was now or never. He feinted to the left, moving the backpack in the same direction, and the Jaguar countered immediately, his reflexes superb, spearing the blade at the pack. At that instant Bolan reversed, going right, letting go of the backpack as he whipped the stiletto around and in, burying the slender dagger in his foe's thigh.

The Jaguar stiffened and grimaced, his upturned face ghostly pale in the subdued moonlight.

In that suspended moment of time, Bolan struck, sliding in close, letting go of the stiletto and executing a right uppercut with all the power in his arm and shoulder, throwing his entire body into the punch. The blow connected squarely on the Jaguar's chin and lifted the man from his feet, crunching teeth and causing blood to spurt from his mouth.

Frantically the Jaguar tried to regain his balance, even as he swung his blade at the big man's face.

Bolan blocked the wild swing with his left forearm, then drove his right fist into the Jaguar's nose. He followed through with two rapid roundhouses that snapped the assassin's head right and left.

Stubbornly the Jaguar stayed on his feet although he tottered unsteadily. His arms sagged. Blood flowed from his crushed nostrils and lips.

The warrior distinctly heard the whoops of the natives. They would be there in sixty seconds. He gripped the Jaguar's right wrist, held fast when the enforcer feebly resisted and bent the man's arm at the elbow. His muscles rippling, he swept the arm upward and sank the blade into the Jaguar's throat.

Bolan released his grip and dashed to his pack. In two bounds he reclaimed it and was off down the trail, looking back to see the Jaguar wrench the blade out and stumble to his knees. A pathetic whine gurgled from the killer's ruptured throat as he tried to stem the blood flow with his left hand. The last Bolan saw of the infamous killer in black, just before turning a curve in the trail, was the Jaguar pitching forward onto his face.

The Executioner pumped his legs into high gear and raced back along the trail, noting certain trees and bushes whose location he'd memorized earlier. To his rear the night air vibrated with the strident cries of the Indians. Any second now they would discover the body. He allowed half a minute, a minute at the most, before they would be in hot pursuit, not much of a margin at all considering how fast they could travel through the jungle.

Bolan scanned both sides for a particular oval-shaped bush. Near it would be his hardware.

There was no doubt when the Teremembes reached the Jaguar. Their shouts became a confused jumble of outraged sentiments, rising in volume as they worked themselves into a frenzy.

The warrior slowed, expecting to see the bush. From where he'd slain the Jaguar to the spot where the enforced had jumped out of the tree wasn't all that far. The guns should be right up ahead.

Like the baying of a pack of bloodhounds, the Indians voiced their collective fury and flowed in pursuit.

He spotted the bush and searched the grass for his weapons. The M-16 was easy to find, but the Beretta and the big .44 took a bit longer. The handguns went into their respective holsters, then he shrugged into the backpack, hefted the rifle and was off at full speed, sticking to the trail for another hundred yards.

The warrior angled sharply to the right, dashing into the jungle and proceeding a mere twenty feet. He crouched behind a tree and ensured his weapons were fully loaded. Peering around the trunk, he waited. His survival depended on how well the Indians could track by the light of the moon. If they noticed where he left the trail, they'd be on him before he could hope to escape. If not, he had a plan worth trying.

Soon the voices seemed to shake the leaves, and the Indians appeared off to the left, running two and three abreast, armed with spears, bows and clubs.

Bolan tensed as they neared his turnoff point, then nodded in satisfaction when the leaders kept racing along the trail. He counted thirty-seven, all told, before the Teremembes vanished into the night, still yelling up a storm.

The warrior rose and moved swiftly to the northeast again, staying within sight of the trail, treading stealthily. Before long he came within sight of the Jaguar's corpse and three men.

Harmodio Remón knelt beside the brother he had developed into the perfect assassin. His head was bowed, his shoulders slumped, his hands resting on the Jaguar's back.

Behind Remón, standing in respectful silence, were two Teremembe warriors, both armed with spears, both watching sadly.

Bolan crept toward them. His job would be easier if he simply shot the Indians, but he still refused to harm them if at all possible. And since he didn't want them to call out and alert the war party, he had to do this the hard way.

Remón looked up at the natives and spoke in their tongue. One of them responded at length, then turned and headed toward the village.

Too bad they both didn't go, Bolan reflected, bent over as he pressed through some high weeds, approaching the remaining Indian from the rear. He adopted a painstaking routine. Take a step and pause. Take a step and pause. If the Indian's head moved, he froze until certain the Teremembe hadn't heard him.

Harmodio Remón ran a hand over his brother's head, sighed and stood.

Bolan eased lower, using the vegetation as a screen. The drug lord and the Indian conversed for a minute, then Remón took a few strides to the southwest and angrily shook his fist while mouthing a string of curses in Spanish. The last word he uttered was "Belasko."

The warrior saw his chance. Both men had their backs to him. He uncoiled and leaped from concealment, drawing the M-16 back, the stock toward the Indian.

Already the Teremembe was starting to turn.

Bolan swung the rifle into the side of the Indian's head, above the ear, the stock thudding solidly and dropping the Teremembe like a rock. His right hand swept to the Beretta, the barrel clearing leather as Harmodio Remón spun. He aimed at the top of the drug lord's nose.

"You!" Remón blurted.

"Me," Bolan said, and fired.

The slug snapped Remón's head back. His legs buckled, and he fell in slow motion until he rested on his side, his mouth open, his eyes fixed blankly on eternity.

Replacing the Beretta, the Executioner glanced to the left, in the direction the lone Indian went, and saw an empty stretch of trail. He glanced to the right and was surprised to see four Teremembes appear. Perhaps they were part of the main war party, returning for some reason. It hardly mattered. The instant they laid eyes on him they vented harsh yells and charged.

Whirling, Bolan plunged into the undergrowth and ran as if running a marathon. In a way he was, a marathon of death with four furies on his heels. At least it wasn't the entire war party. He might be able to lose the quartet if he could outdistance them.

A long, slender arrow whizzed out of the night and smacked into a tree within a foot of the warrior's head.

Bolan weaved, presenting an elusive target, hoping there weren't any poisonous snakes in his path. He covered several hundred yards before he looked back to see if he'd shaken them.

There they were, thirty yards away, their pale faces revealed against the backdrop of dark vegetation.

He tried to discourage them with a short burst into the trees above their heads, but the quartet never slowed. Under different circumstances he might have admired their persistence. Now he wished they weren't so brave, and resumed his flight.

Minutes went by. Sweat caked Bolan from head to toe. The outline of a high hill materialized ahead and gave him cause for hope. He passed under a towering tree, swatted at dangling vines that barred his path, and felt a huge spider scramble onto his neck.

Bolan couldn't stop. He continued running toward the hill with the spider perched on the right side of his neck, above the collar. It was an enormous specimen with a leg spread of six or seven inches, and only one type of spider grew that large—the tarantula. Specifically the tarantula commonly known as the bird spider, a tree-dwelling variety that hunted small birds for food.

The good news was that they weren't poisonous. However, their bites were intensely painful, sometimes requiring prolonged bed rest before complete recovery.

Bolan could feel his hairy legs pressing against his skin. He expected to experience the sharp pain of its fangs sinking into his flesh at any second, but it seemed content simply to go along for the ride. Perhaps its instincts told it not to antagonize something Bolan's size. Whatever, he had to get rid of it fast. He didn't dare turn his head to check on the Indians with the thing clinging there.

The warrior transferred the M-16 to his left hand, still running at top speed, and reached up until his fingers were almost touching the arachnid hitchhiker. He plucked the squat body from his neck, flinging it aside in a blur of motion. Relief washed over him like a refreshing cold shower. Very fleeting relief.

Another arrow flashed from the rear and buzzed past his head.

A quick glance verified the four shadows were still on his tail. He came to the bottom of the hill and started upward, searching for the ideal spot to implement his plan. Halfway to the summit he found it, a circular clearing twenty feet in diameter. He plunged into the brush beyond, traveling fifty feet before stopping next to a log and turning. He quickly fed a high-explosive round into the M-203.

The leading pair of Teremembes appeared at the far side of the clearing, their companions close behind.

Bolan let them get a third of the way across before he fired, aiming at a point off to the left, far enough away not to injure the Indians but close enough to give them a healthy scare.

All four abruptly halted when the blast rocked the jungle. They gestured and spoke excitedly.

The warrior gave them more to talk about, a buck-shot can off to the right. The second explosion almost did the trick.

Three of the Indians began to flee when the fourth said something that rooted them in place.

Bolan grasped a smoke grenade. He deftly lobbed it into the clearing and saw it roll toward the Teremembes, smoke pouring from the four holes in its top.

The quartet took one look and bolted, fleeing like terrified deer.

For the first time in many hours Bolan smiled. Pivoting, he climbed to the top of the hill and paused to inhale the muggy air. He doubted the Indians would stop until they reached their village, and the tale they told would deter others from pursuing him. All he had to do now was check the radio, and if it worked he'd be on his way back to the States by daylight.

One battle was over, but the war would go on. The warrior set the backpack on the ground and bent to retrieve the radio.

**Raw determination
in a dark new age.**

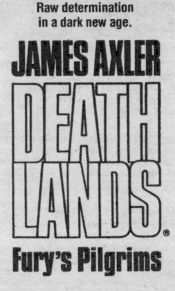

JAMES AXLER
DEATH LANDS®
Fury's Pilgrims

A bad jump from a near-space Gateway leaves Ryan Cawdor and his band of warrior survivalists in the devastated heart of the American Midwest. In a small community that was once the sprawling metropolis of Chicago, Krysty is taken captive by a tribe of nocturnal female mutants. Ryan fears for her life, especially since she is a woman.

In the Deathlands, life is a contest where the only victor is death.

Gold Eagle brings another fast-paced miniseries to the action adventure front!

by PATRICK F. ROGERS

Omega Force: the last—and deadliest—option

With capabilities unmatched by any other paramilitary organization in the world, Omega Force is a special ready-reaction antiterrorist strike force composed of the best commandos and equipment the military has to offer.

In Book 1: **WAR MACHINE,** two dozen SCUDs have been smuggled into Libya by a secret Iraqi extremist group whose plan is to exact ruthless retribution in the Middle East. The President has no choice but to call in Omega Force—a swift and lethal way to avert World War III.

The year is 2030 and the world is in a state of political and territorial unrest. The Peacekeepers, an elite military force, will not negotiate for peace—they're ready to impose it with the ultimate in 21st-century weaponry.

2030

by MICHAEL KASNER

Introducing the follow-up miniseries to the WARKEEP 2030 title published in November 1992.

In Book 1: **KILLING FIELDS**, the Peacekeepers join forces with spear-throwing Zulus as violence erupts in black-ruled South Africa—violence backed by money, fanaticism and four neutron bombs.

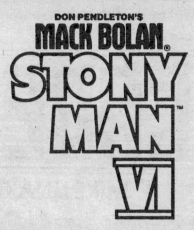